With Every Step, the Snow Became More Blinding.

She could see only a few feet ahead. Now she was heading into the wind, which had suddenly picked up speed. What if she wasn't going southwest anymore? She longed to be home; she wouldn't turn back. Addie stopped to wrap her scarf over her mouth and nose to make it easier to breathe. She rubbed her eyes with her mittens to brush away ice that clung to her lashes and froze her eyelids shut.

. . . How could she ever find her way home? She reached out her arms. She groped in the wind and snow. Nothing. Her eyes were freezing shut again. She rubbed them with her mittens and kept walking.

ADDIE'S DAKOTA WINTER

LAURIE LAWLOR

Illustrated by Toby Gowing

A MINSTREL® BOOK

PUBLISHED BY POCKET BOOKS

New York   London   Toronto   Sydney   Tokyo   Singapore

For my parents

The lines on page 47 are from "The Day Is Done" by Henry Wadsworth Longfellow. The lines on page 53 are from McGuffey's *Third Eclectic Reader*.

A Minstrel Book published by
POCKET BOOKS, a division of Simon & Schuster Inc.
1230 Avenue of the Americas, New York, NY 10020

Text copyright © 1989 by Laurie Lawlor
Illustrations copyright © 1989 by Toby Gowing

Published by arrangement with Albert Whitman & Company

ISBN: 0-671-70148-7

First Minstrel Books printing December 1991

10 9 8 7 6

A MINSTREL BOOK and colophon are registered trademarks of Simon & Schuster Inc.

Cover art by Diane Sivavec

Printed in the U.S.A.

Contents

1 FIRST DAY OF SCHOOL

Addie shielded her eyes from the sun's glare and searched the boundless Dakota horizon for a sign of her slow-moving brother. Whenever she paused to see if nine-year-old George was still following her, he seemed farther and farther behind. This time he had disappeared altogether.

"George, where are you?" she shouted.

No answer.

The wind made the golden-grey Indian grass covering a low hill rise and fall suddenly, as if an enormous, unseen giant, deep in the loamy black underground, had just rolled over in his sleep.

Addie took a deep breath. There were no child-eating giants living inside the prairie, except in stories she made up for three-year-old Burt, five-year-old Lew, and year-old Nellie May. Addie told those stories just to frighten her younger brothers and sister. Now she had frightened herself. Her heart pounded.

"George!" she yelled, her voice anxious. "If you make me late for our first day of school, I'll never forgive you!"

No answer.

What if he's just out of sight, laughing at me? Addie thought. She slammed her lunch pail on the ground. All right. She'd show him. She'd stand right here and wait. He'd have to come out of hiding sometime, wouldn't he?

Impatiently, Addie folded her arms and thought about how much she really disliked her brother. He was bossy, boastful, and unpleasant. He cheated in games so that he always won. He played mean tricks on Lew and Burt when Mother wasn't looking. And she knew for absolute certain that he had once tried to smoke a piece of clothesline behind the outhouse.

"Good riddance!" she shouted, grabbing her lunch pail and stomping toward school. She hoped he *was* gone forever.

She stopped. Her shoulders slumped. Mother had told Addie that George was her responsibility. She was supposed to make sure her brother arrived at school on time and in fairly tidy condition. "George hasn't been to school before, the way you have. See that he behaves," Mother confided when George was out of earshot. "If he sits still long enough and keeps out of trouble, perhaps he'll learn to read."

Now George would never learn to read because he was

lost — gone forever. What would Mother say when Addie told her the bad news? And how could she explain to Pa the way George had disappeared on their two-mile walk? No one would believe that he had simply dropped off the face of the earth somewhere between the creek bed and the telegraph poles. Her parents would blame Addie for being careless. It would be all her fault. And what about her poor brother? Addie imagined him wandering on the open prairie for days and nights, cold and hungry and afraid.

"George Sidney Mills!" she screamed as loud as she could. "Answer me, this minute!"

A familiar brown cap bobbed up through the tall grass. The cap came closer. Addie did not know whether to be happy or angry to see her brother's disgusted face.

"Why are you screaming?" George complained, scratching his forehead. Was this all he had to look forward to now that school started? Day in day out, women forever yelling at him? First his mother ordering him to wear clean clothes. Then his sister shouting for him to hurry. Next would be his teacher — what awful, shrill kind of screaming would she do? These thoughts made George so mad that he gave the tall grass an enormous kick. Frantic grasshoppers leapt out of his way.

"Why didn't you answer me? We're late. Don't you want to get to school on time?"

"Nope," he replied sullenly, and ripped a grass stalk to

chew. With his dirty fingernail, he slit the tough casing away and put the tender end in his mouth. "Just as soon never get there at all."

Addie stared at her stubborn brother. How could he feel that way? She could hardly wait to go back to school after being out a whole year, ever since her family had come to Dakota from Sabula, Iowa, in 1883. Until this fall, there had been no school for the children of Hutchinson County. Now the county finally had its own schoolhouse. It wasn't just the poems and the penmanship and the sums that Addie longed to practice again. What she wanted most of all was to make a friend.

Because her family had been so busy their first year homesteading at Oak Hollow, Addie and George hadn't met or played with any other children. There had been a sod house and barn to build and fields to plow, plant, cultivate, and harvest. Sunup to sundown, as soon as one chore was finished, another waited to be started. Even Lew and Burt had jobs. They helped scare away hungry blackbirds, weed the onions, and pinch bugs off the cucumber and melon vines. Luckily, the weather had cooperated throughout the growing season. A bumper crop of flax — fibrous plants that were used for coarse cloth and rope — had been sold for cash in the nearest town, Scotland. Corn and vegetables had been canned in jars and stood row upon row in the Mills' root cellar. The family would not have to eat meal after meal of salt pork and beans, the way they had their first winter on the prairie.

At school there would be no babies to watch, no laundry to hang, no water to haul, no stiff, dry grass to twist into tight bundles called hay cats for the potbelly stove. And best of all, Hutchinson County's schoolhouse was bound to have other girls exactly ten years old. Didn't Pa say there were new settlers taking up claims nearly every day?

Why, Addie had even seen a girl her age near the salt-pork kegs at Schlissman's store in Scotland last spring. The girl reminded Addie of Eleanor, the best friend she had left behind in Iowa. Too shy to speak, Addie kept her distance, but she memorized everything about the stranger. All the long way home, Addie thought about the girl's mischievous smile, her proper crinoline apron, and her fair hair braided neatly with a pale purple ribbon. Wouldn't it be fine if the stranger were in her class?

While taking care of Burt, Lew, and little Nellie May, Addie often imagined the games she and her new schoolmate would play, all the secrets they would share. She even imagined her new friend's name — Annabelle. It was the most perfect name Addie could think of. And why not? Annabelle never quarreled or lied or bragged or acted mean. She spoke in a gentle voice and had very good manners. And she enjoyed playing make-believe, just like Addie.

Addie was so certain that Annabelle would be at school that she had brought her most precious belonging just to show her. Ruby Lillian, a smiling, china-head doll no bigger than Addie's hand, was hiding safely inside her apron pocket. The doll had been given to Addie one year ago by Anna Fency, a neighboring homesteader who had befriended the Mills family when they came to Dakota. Ruby Lillian's features and brown ringlets were painted. The doll's body was only stuffed cotton. But her bright eyes, soft cupid's-bow mouth, and blushing cheeks seemed so real to Addie that sometimes she thought she could see Ruby Lillian breathe.

Addie took good care of Ruby Lillian and guarded her from her brothers, who often had dirty hands and nasty ideas when it came to dolls. Ruby Lillian slept in her own tiny cigar-box bed on a mattress filled with downy milkweed tufts. The dainty blue-gingham dress she wore had been stitched specially by Addie for this important day, their first day of school.

George belched loudly, startling Addie. He smiled with pleasure to see her look of total disapproval.

"How rude! You better not do that in school."

"Why not?" he said in a mocking voice. Why did his sister have to be such a goody-goody?

"Because you'll get in trouble, that's why."

George looked unimpressed.

"And if you get in trouble all the time, you won't learn anything," she warned. "Don't you want to learn something important? Don't you want to learn to read?"

"Nope."

"Don't you want to learn how to do sums?"

"Nope."

She stopped in her tracks and swung around to face him. "You want to be ignorant your whole life?"

George took the grass out of his mouth and spat on the ground, just like a grown-up man. His stupid sister didn't seem to understand how much he hated the idea of being trapped inside a stuffy, boring classroom all day when he might be outside doing something interesting. He would rather hunt prairie chickens or fish for bullheads. He'd rather help Pa fix the fence or break a new colt. He'd rather be outdoors where he could breathe and run and yell if he felt like it, and where there wasn't any teacher to tell him to sit down and be quiet. What difference did it make if he ever learned to read? "School's a plain waste of time," he replied angrily, "and don't you dare call me ignorant."

Addie rolled her eyes in exasperation and started walking again. George was hopeless. She wished Mother hadn't made her new apron and George's new shirt from the same bolt of turkey-red calico. Now her classmates would know right away that this rude, horrible boy was her brother.

They walked silently side by side, shouldering into the wind like fish swimming upstream. After a whole year in Dakota, Addie still had not grown accustomed to this invisible force that moved restlessly across the treeless prairie, turning each blade of grass as if there might be something hidden underneath. The weather here was always windier than Addie remembered in Sabula, which was sheltered by Mississippi bluffs. Pa joked that Dakota was nine months of winter, three months of wind, and the rest summer.

Addie knew that like the wind, Dakota's unpredictable weather was part of their new life. Before she and George had left for school, Mother had warned them to watch the sky for the sudden appearance of heavy, dark grey clouds. "If it looks like snow when it's time to come home, you both stay at school and Pa will come for you."

Addie sniffed the late October air. It smelled grassy and clean. The bright sun felt warm. Winter seemed a long way off. She looked up and examined the white clouds that dragged along in the vast blue sky. They all had dusty purple undersides, like the smudged bottoms of bare feet. These weren't snow clouds, she knew that much.

"What's for lunch?" George asked, poking inside his lunch pail.

"Mother packed some very nice butter sandwiches. Don't eat them now or you'll be hungry the rest of the day."

Her brother took out a piece of bread, folded it in half, stuffed it into his mouth, and chewed noisily. He walked more slowly now that he could actually see the school in the distance.

The stark white building had been constructed with money collected from many families in Hutchinson County. It stood without a bush or fence or tree to hide behind. To Addie, the schoolhouse and the nearby shed and outhouse of tar paper and pine boards looked out of place. On the wide-open prairie, sod houses crouched, camouflaged and sturdy. But these new buildings appeared fragile and helpless, ready at any moment to be swept away by the wind or gulped by a giant.

She peered at faraway children running and chasing each other and listened to their shouting. The sounds reminded her of the schoolyard back in Sabula. Were the girls her age here yet? She scanned the crowd for Annabelle. Her stomach fluttered like a windflower in a spring storm. She put her hand in her pocket and held Ruby Lillian very tightly.

In a few moments, they would reach the point of no return. She and George would be inside the school.

What if she couldn't remember anything she had learned in Sabula? What if she had forgotten all the tutoring Anna Fency had provided last winter? The other children might laugh and make fun of her. "I don't...I don't feel so good," Addie said slowly.

15

"Now what's the matter?" George demanded. He was watching a group of boys throwing a rag ball over the outhouse roof. The game looked very interesting.

"Maybe going to school isn't such a good idea after all. Maybe I should go home. You know, they need us. Mother's going to have a hard time getting anything done without somebody to watch Nellie May and Burt and Lew," Addie mumbled. But she wasn't really thinking about her overworked mother or her bothersome sister or brothers. She was worried about the teacher she had never laid eyes on before. She imagined an old, cruel woman with long, clawlike fingers. The woman's teeth were sharp and yellow, and she had hot, sour breath. "I think I want to go home," she said in a small, frightened voice.

"Oh, Addie, come on! I want to try that game. Do you think those big boys would let me play?"

Before she could answer, someone rang a loud bell. The crowd of children raced to the door.

"Run, Addie, run!" George cried, leaping and skipping like the other boys. He grabbed her hand and dragged her to the end of the line of children being swallowed up inside the schoolhouse.

17

2   A SOMETIME FRIEND

The new teacher stood in the schoolroom doorway. Looking straight into her face required more courage than Addie could muster. Instead, when it was her turn to walk through the door, she purposefully kept her eyes down. She stared nervously at her teacher's hands.

To her surprise, they were neither gnarled nor clawlike. They were freckled and lively. These were practical hands that were used to hard work. When Addie looked up, she saw that her teacher was quite young and barely as tall as some of the boys who shuffled reluctantly into class. She wore a pale blue dress with a pretty lace collar. Her wavy, reddish brown hair was piled on the top of her head. When she greeted each pupil, her black eyes danced.

She smiled and shook Addie's hand. "Good morning," she said in a pleasant way.

Addie was so pleased that she could not think of anything

to say. She was aware of a faint fragrance in the air, like the wild roses that grew down by the slough in June. As she hurried with George to an empty bench, she hastily sniffed her own hand. The scent of wild roses lingered there. Not only did her new teacher seem friendly, she smelled good. Addie was glad, after all, that she had not run home.

Addie gazed around the room, which still carried the scent of lime whitewash and new wood. Stubborn green grass poked between the rough floorboards. A potbelly stove squatted in the middle of the room. A black pipe ran from the stove to the ceiling, where it connected to the smokestack on the roof. On either side of the stove was a row of ten crude wooden benches.

Fifteen pegs for coats and hats had been hammered into the wall near the door. There was a tin dipper hanging above a pail of drinking water. Nearby on an old keg sat a chunk of lye soap and an empty tin basin for washing hands.

Addie counted four windows, two on the east wall and two on the west. In the front of the classroom was the teacher's desk, nothing more than a plank of wood between two sawhorses. Atop the plank was a black notebook, a wooden ruler, a pair of wire-rimmed reading glasses, and a bunch of sky-blue asters in a jelly jar of water.

Where was the blackboard? Where was the roll-down map of North America? She remembered that the Sabula schoolhouse also had a picture of grim President Washington and an American flag hanging from the wall. There was nothing like that here, but the buzz of excited children talking was very familiar. "Good morning to all of you," the teacher said in a loud voice. "Please take your seats."

"Good morning, ma'am," some of the children echoed. A group of big boys remained standing in the back of the room, hooting and poking at one another.

"Gentlemen, please take your seats. Now, I want everyone to be as comfortable as possible. We are hoping to have real desks soon. As you can see, our accommodations here are quite Spartan, but we will do the best we can."

When the boys at the back of the room ignored her request, the teacher continued as if they weren't there. "My name is Miss Elizabeth Brophy, and I am your teacher for this term. Now I will call the roll. Please answer when you hear your name so that I do not mark you absent."

Addie carefully smoothed her new apron. She made sure that Ruby Lillian was still in her pocket. The disrespectful big boys in the back of the room made her nervous. What if one of them got hold of her doll? She studied Miss Brophy's kind face. Would her teacher be able to control the bullies? Addie decided to help Miss Brophy as best she could by listening attentively.

George did not want to listen. He twisted around in

his seat and stared. Why, there were more children in this room than he had seen in one place in over a year. And look at those big boys! They weren't doing anything they were told to do, and they weren't even being punished. One of them barked like a dog. George smiled. Maybe school would be more fun than he had thought.

"Turn around and wipe that silly grin off your face, George!" Addie whispered. She jabbed her brother hard so he would know she was serious.

Miss Brophy ignored the barking. She cleared her throat, put on her glasses, and read from the class list inside her notebook: "Fred Falkenberg."

"Here I am."

"Donald Feeney."

"Here."

"Lorenzo and Lucia Hebbert?"

"We're right here," said Lucia. "I'm eight years old."

Addie tried to memorize each new name, all the while searching for Annabelle. She learned that sitting on the bench directly behind her were Arnold and Simon Shaver — two small, dirty boys — and their unhappy-looking teenaged brother named Conrad. All three brothers had the same hard, bright eyes and wore the same kind of flour-sack shirt.

She studied the four other girls in the class, all too young and all decidedly unappealing. Lucia Hebbert kept scratching her scruffy braids. Addie wondered if Lucia had lice and decided to make a special point of avoiding her. Maude and Lucy Hoopes were skinny twin sisters. When the teacher asked their ages, they shyly refused to talk. Addie guessed they might be seven and wondered if they only spoke to each other. Scrappy Myra Renshaw in filthy overalls blurted out that she was six years old and could beat up anybody.

The boys lurking in the back of the room laughed and jeered at Myra. Their names were Malcolm Connolly, Tommy Owens, and Herbert Bradbury. The tallest, meanest-looking boy was sixteen-year-old Malcolm. Malcolm's thick brown hair stood in unruly tufts, his neck was the color of dirty water, and his grin was unfriendly. Surly Tommy and Herbert volunteered that they were fifteen years old. They imitated the way Malcolm leaned, his back against the wall, his knee bent, and his big boot heel pressed firmly on the fresh whitewash.

Just then a whole new crowd of students burst through the doorway. Addie turned around for a better look.

"Please come in and sit down!" Miss Brophy said, pointing to a bench.

Half a dozen frightened and confused-looking children of all ages pushed their way inside and sat on the very last bench huddled shoulder to shoulder, as if they might be safer that way. Their clothing was unlike anything Addie had ever seen before. They had strange wooden shoes. Instead of sunbonnets, the girls wore black kerchiefs on their heads. Their enormous, queer, old dresses had frayed sleeves and collars and looked as if they had belonged to their mothers. In spite of the warm autumn weather, the biggest boy kept on a huge overcoat that looked as if it had been sewn from a horse blanket. Three younger boys in ragged jackets pulled their squashed caps down over their ears.

"Please tell us your names," Miss Brophy said, her pencil poised. "I don't seem to have you on my list."

The boy in the big overcoat stood, took off his cap, and twisted it.

"What are your names?" Miss Brophy repeated.

The boy turned bright red, his eyes never leaving the floor. Someone giggled.

"Do you speak English?"

The littlest girl began to whisper nervously. She tried to run out the door, but her older sister grabbed her.

"Ya. Ve speak a leetle," the boy said finally, still twisting his cap.

"They're Rooshens," shouted Malcolm. "But you can't get them to talk nothing but German. Anybody knows that."

"What is your name?" Miss Brophy asked kindly.

"Schuler." He pointed to himself and then to each of the other newcomers. "Gunther, Rolfe, Emile, Rudolph, Emma, and Lena."

"You are Russian?"

"No. Ve are Germans. Ve are Germans living in Russia before ve came here."

"You speak German?"

"Ya."

"We will speak only English in my class. Do you understand?"

Gunther nodded but still seemed confused. He sat down beside Emma, who looked as if she might be at least fourteen.

Too old, Addie decided. And she can't even speak English. Addie sighed with disappointment. There was no one here she wanted to share Ruby Lillian with, no one at all.

"How many of you already know how to read?" Miss Brophy asked.

Shyly, Addie raised her hand. She hoped the teacher would not make her demonstrate by reading aloud something difficult. When she turned to see how many others had raised their hands, she was surprised to spot only Fred Falkenberg and Donald Feeney. She was less ignorant than she had feared.

"Please don't stand outside," Miss Brophy said, motioning to someone hovering in the doorway. You can sit up here in the front row with Addie and George."

A willow-thin girl with pale blue eyes and pale yellow hair placed a piece of paper on Miss Brophy's desk and slid silently onto the bench next to Addie. While Miss Brophy read the paper, Addie had a chance to take a good look at this new girl. Even sitting straight and tall, her chin lifted proudly — almost stubbornly — she did not appear to be any older than nine. A wrinkled blue kerchief was tied around her head.

"Did your parents write this for you?" Miss Brophy asked.

The girl shook her head, as if deeply embarrassed.

"You wrote this yourself?"

The girl nodded, folding and unfolding a corner of her worn, embroidered apron. She glanced at her lap, as if she were trying to regain her confidence there among the faded stitched flowers.

"Can you tell the class your name?"

The girl looked up and in a loud sing-song voice said, "My name Mathilde Bergstrom."

"All right, I will add you to our list of pupils, Mathilde."

"Tilla," the girl corrected her.

"Tilla, your penmanship is quite excellent. Did you copy this from a newspaper?"

Tilla nodded enthusiastically. "I practice English."

"Can you read?"

"You mean *riksmaal* — Norwegian book words?"

"No, I mean English. Can you read English?"

Tilla shook her head, ashamed.

25

"Well, then, you shall have plenty of company. Nearly all of you will be learning to read this year," Miss Brophy said cheerfully. She looked directly at Addie. "Those who know how can assist me."

Addie felt a warm glow of importance.

"You won't teach *me* anything," announced Malcolm. The other boys had finally taken their seats, but Malcolm was still in the back of the room, leaning against the wall.

"Please sit down so that we can begin our lesson. And kindly refrain from damaging the whitewash," Miss Brophy said sternly. "And Malcolm — where is your brother?"

"Out," he said with a smirk.

"Out where?"

"Outside."

Miss Brophy went to the door. Suddenly, the boy everyone knew must be Malcolm's brother appeared in the window. He looked like a coyote peering into a henhouse. Grinning, he pulled himself inside, and everyone laughed.

"I do not find this amusing," Miss Brophy said. "The door — not the window — is to be used for entrance into this classroom."

Daniel joined his barrel-chested brother in slouching against the wall. He was smaller and thinner than Malcolm, but every bit as bold and swaggering. The boys took large pinches from a shared pouch of tobacco and began chewing.

George watched, spellbound. The only people he'd ever seen use tobacco before were grown men. The Connolly brothers' daring made George feel frightened and full of admiration all at the same time. Addie noticed her brother staring with awe at Malcolm and Daniel, and she kicked him.

Miss Brophy continued, "Until our McGuffey Readers arrive, we will practice the alphabet."

Addie did not understand why Miss Brophy was ignoring the tobacco chewing. Was she going to discipline the Connolly brothers after school? She hoped that her teacher knew best. Meanwhile, the boys in the back of the room moved their jaws like contented cows in spring clover.

Miss Brophy held up a piece of pine board and with a stick of charcoal made a large letter. "Please repeat after me," she said. "A is for apple."

"A is for apple," the class thundered.

"B is for bear," Miss Brophy said, scratching another letter.

Addie's mind wandered. This girl from Norway sitting next to her did not look anything like the friend she was waiting for. Tilla did not speak correct English. She wore foreign-looking clothes. Her proud eyes seemed to be laughing defiantly at the whole world, as if to say, "I may be little and scrawny, but I'm not afraid of anything."

"D is for Dog!" echoed the other children's deafening shout.

She's not like Annabelle, not one bit, Addie decided. Why, Tilla did not even have eyelashes or eyebrows like a proper American girl. Or were her eyebrows so pale blonde that they just seemed invisible?

Addie shot a glance in Tilla's direction, just to make sure. She was startled to find the Norwegian girl examining her, just as curiously. Addie couldn't help herself. She smiled. Tilla looked quickly away, but there was a faint shadow of a grin on her face, too.

Maybe, Addie thought, this strange girl from Norway could be her *sometime* friend — just until a *real* friend came along. She might even invite Tilla to her house on a Saturday morning, if it was all right with Mother. Perhaps Mother could make them a special picnic lunch, just the way she did in Sabula when Eleanor came to play.

Of course, Tilla wasn't anything like Eleanor — or Annabelle. Tilla really didn't count. She could share picnic lunches, but she could not share secrets. Only someone as perfect as Annabelle could share Ruby Lillian. Until that perfect friend walked through the schoolroom door, Ruby Lillian would have to remain hidden. Addie patted the china-head doll hiding patiently inside her dark apron pocket.

3 GINGERBREAD
AND MAKE-BELIEVE

One Saturday afternoon, three weeks after school had begun, Addie sat on the soddy roof holding her squirmy baby sister. She was trying to keep Nellie May out of trouble while Mother boiled sheets outdoors in a kettle over a fire. The weather was still unseasonably warm, and Mother wanted to get as much laundry done as possible.

Addie had tried singing songs to entertain Nellie May. She had tried telling stories. But Nellie May wasn't interested.

Nellie May did not look the way Addie imagined a baby girl should. She was nearly bald. She did not act the way Addie imagined a baby girl should, either. She enjoyed nothing better than playing rough-and-tumble with her wild brothers. Whenever Addie tried to play "Going Visiting" and "Tea Party," Nellie May refused to be dressed up. Instead, she

29

tore off her bonnet and ate the clumps of mud that were supposed to be tea cakes.

Addie and Nellie May could hear Burt and Lew on the ground below shooting at each other with sticks. "Guts!" Nellie yelled the horrible word her brothers had taught her. They ignored her.

"You're dead!" Lew shouted, aiming his stick at Burt.

"Am not!" Burt replied. He galloped about on a broom handle.

"Are too!"

"Am not!"

"Guts! Guts!" Nellie screamed, louder this time.

"Sit down, Nellie! And stop saying that bad word," Addie said crossly, grabbing her sister before she scrambled too close to the edge of the roof. Addie did not want to take care of Nellie May. She had more important things on her mind. She stood with the stubborn, wriggling toddler on one hip and stared into the distance.

Where was Tilla? It was already past noon. On Friday, she had promised she would come to Addie's house the next morning. Addie had drawn careful directions on a piece of brown paper. She showed Tilla exactly how to get to Oak Hollow from the schoolhouse by walking south, past the telegraph poles and the railroad tracks, over the low rise, around the buffalo wallow, and across Choteau Creek.

Addie waited all morning. Had Tilla broken her promise? Was she lost?

"Addie, don't let the boys get too close to the kettle," Mother called. "I'm going inside. Do you see your friend yet?"

"No," Addie replied. She felt so disappointed.

"I'm sure she'll be here." Mother said.

Addie sniffed the air. The sweet, spicy smell of gingerbread floated temptingly out of the open door below. Mother had not made gingerbread since they had left Sabula. No one was allowed to go into the soddy until the baking was finished.

The gingerbread was Mother's treat to celebrate the arrival of Addie's guest. What if Tilla didn't come? Addie thought miserably. She would miss the gingerbread. She would miss everything.

"Look out! I've got you this time," Burt screamed.

"I shot you first," Lew replied. The two boys wrestled each other, rolling over and over in the dirt.

Nellie watched and whimpered. She scurried backwards on her hands and knees toward the ladder. She wanted to climb off the roof.

"Oh, all right, Nellie, let's go down. But you can't fight with the boys," Addie told her sister. One last time, she gazed to the north where Pa and George were plowing. There, she saw a small shape struggling closer. Addie watched. The shape grew bigger. Addie rubbed her eyes. The shape was someone with two heads! How could that be? In another minute Addie was able to see a small person carrying a smaller person, piggyback. "Tilla! Tilla!" Addie shouted and waved from the rooftop.

The shape waved back.

Addie held Nellie tightly with one arm and scrambled down the ladder. Nellie made complaining noises as Addie leapt through the tall, dry grass. "Tilla! Tilla!" Addie called breathlessly. She was surprised at how happy she suddenly felt.

"Hello!" Tilla called back. Her face was flushed and sweaty. She was carrying a small, pretty girl with pale blue eyes, just like Tilla's, and a halo of long blonde curls that went every which way.

"Who's this?"

"My sister. Say *god dag*, Katya," Tilla replied. Katya buried her face in the back of her big sister's neck. "Had to bring her. Sorry."

"That's all right. I have to watch Nellie May, too. We can take care of them together. Then it won't be so bad." Nellie reached over and pinched Katya's fat, bare foot. "Be nice, Nellie May," Addie ordered, deciding she wouldn't mind trading sisters with Tilla. At least Tilla's sister looked like a girl.

Carrying their little sisters, Tilla and Addie walked slowly toward the soddy. Suddenly, Addie could not think of anything to say. She was embarrassed. What if Tilla didn't like her house? What if she thought Lew and Burt were awful? What if she didn't care for Mother's gingerbread? This was the first time Addie had invited anyone to her home since she had come to Dakota. Tilla's opinion mattered, even though she was just a temporary friend.

"Who's she?" Lew demanded rudely, pointing at Tilla and then stuffing his fists into his pockets. His face was covered with dirty smears. Behind him stood Burt, looking just as filthy. He scowled at the visitors and scratched under his arm.

"This is Tilla and her sister Katya. Tilla goes to school with me. Mother's making us a special picnic and you both better leave us alone," Addie warned.

"How many broders you got?" Tilla asked, shifting Katya to the opposite arm.

"Three," Addie replied. "Three too many."

Tilla laughed. "I got six. Six too many."

Now it was Addie's turn to laugh. They understood each other. Having too many brothers was a miserable experience neither girl had to explain.

"Also I got tree sisters," Tilla added. "Two big and dis little one."

"So is this your friend, Addie?" Mother asked from the doorway, wiping her hands on her apron.

"This is Tilla. And her sister Katya," Addie said.

Tilla made a little curtsy Addie thought was very odd. Was Tilla showing off or was this some kind of Norwegian custom? Apparently Mother did not think Tilla's curtsy was odd. She smiled warmly as if she thought the curtsy was quite charming. "Where do you live?"

"Ve live at Ree Heights," Tilla explained. She pulled from her pocket a stub of pencil and the map Addie had drawn. She quickly added the road that went southeast, past the schoolhouse. She sketched the Jim River, a grove of cottonwood trees, and Ree Heights. "My house right here. Not so far." She showed Mother the map.

"That must be five miles altogether, the way you came. Did you carry your sister the whole time?"

"Ya." Tilla thrust out her proud chin. "I not forget da vay." She tucked the map back into her apron.

"Addie told me that Miss Brophy has been giving you special English lessons after class every day. She says you're learning quickly. You speak very well," Mother said.

Addie could tell that Mother was impressed. She couldn't help feeling a twinge of jealousy. Tilla always impressed grown-ups. Miss Brophy was so taken by Tilla that she even gave her private English lessons and let her borrow books.

Addie wished she could spend as much time with Miss Brophy as Tilla did.

"I just about have your picnic ready," Mother said. "I'm making something I think you'll like."

"Something special," Lew said, sniffing the air eagerly.

Tilla could smell the delightful spices, too. She closed her eyes and took a deep breath.

"Gingerbread! Is it gingerbread?" Burt asked happily.

"We'll see," Mother replied, disappearing inside the soddy.

"Your mudder is very beautiful," Tilla whispered.

Addie looked at Tilla in amazement. No one had ever told her before that her mother was beautiful. She was just a mother. A plain, ordinary mother.

"But not so beautiful like Miss Brophy," Tilla added.

Addie nodded. Anyone could see that. Miss Brophy was in a category all by herself.

"Does your mudder sing?" Tilla asked.

"She knows a few church songs," Addie admitted.

"My mudder sings like bird," Tilla said. "She knows all *Norsk* songs."

Mother came back outside with a basket and a worn blanket. "Here's your lunch, girls. Why don't you eat it by the creek?" she suggested. "You can take the blanket along to sit on."

"But what about the boys?" Addie said. She could see

Lew and Burt lurking around the corner of the soddy. At least George was busy helping Pa in the field. She didn't have to worry about him.

"They won't bother you," Mother said. "They'll be too busy eating their own gingerbread."

Addie and Tilla carried the basket, the blanket, and their two sisters down to Rattling Creek. Although the peach willows and cottonwoods had lost their leaves and the grass was dry and bent, it was a pleasant, sunny picnic spot. Addie spread the blanket. She wished she did not have her disobedient sister along, but it could not be helped. As soon as she put Nellie on the ground, the baby crawled off and began chewing on a stick. Why couldn't she behave like Katya, who did not roam away but instead quietly examined a leaf?

"Now let's see what we have," Addie said. She tried to sound unexcited, as if she were quite accustomed to having special picnic lunches.

Tilla watched eagerly as Addie unwrapped two bread-and-butter sandwiches and two hard-boiled eggs from inside scraps of muslin. She gave Tilla a sandwich and an egg. Tilla marveled at the egg, as if it were a precious treasure.

Addie smiled. She enjoyed impressing her guest. She tapped the egg against her knee, cracked it, and peeled away the shell. "Come and get lunch, Nellie," Addie called. Nellie crawled close and began gnawing on some bread.

Tilla carefully pushed her fingernail into the mid-point of her peeled egg. She ate exactly half and reluctantly gave the rest to her hungry sister. Then Tilla quickly finished the bread and licked her fingers.

"Now for the best part." Addie said. She took two tin cups from the basket and filled them with water from the stream. Carefully, she set them on the blanket. "We can pretend we are fancy ladies having a tea party."

"Fancy?"

"You know — we are queens. We are very rich. We live in castles, and we are visiting each other. See? I'll twist this bunch of grass and make crowns for us," Addie said, quickly braiding strands of tough Indian grass and fastening the ends to make a circle. She placed her crown on her head and made another for Tilla.

Tilla put on the crown and grinned. Now she understood the game.

Addie handed Tilla a cup. "I hope this tea is just the way you like it, my dear."

"Oh, ya!" Tilla replied. She took a sip carefully, as if the cool water from Rattling Creek was very hot tea.

Addie smiled. She could see that Tilla was good at pretending. Daintily, she poured invisible cream and sugar into her cup and stirred with an invisible, elegant silver spoon. Addie lifted the muslin cloth in the basket and discovered a wonderful surprise. Instead of ordinary square-cut gingerbread, Mother had made four gingermen with fat, comical arms and legs and currant eyes and buttons.

"Have a gingerman," Addie said in her most proud, queenly voice. She gave each girl one. "I eat gingermen every day. My royal baker makes me three or four for every meal." Addie admired her fragrant, perfect gingerman, memorizing each feature before she nibbled on his toe.

"So beautiful!" Tilla said and sighed, gazing at her gingerman. Then she closed her eyes and bit off its head. The children ate silently, thoroughly enjoying their treat.

"More!" demanded Nellie. She had savagely crumbled her gingerman and stuffed as much as she could into her mouth at once. Crumbs clung to the front of her dress.

"Nellie, you've already had your share," Addie said. "Why can't you eat slowly and neatly like Katya? At least she has manners like a princess."

"More!" Nellie repeated. She scrambled across the blanket and grabbed Katya's gingerman. Katya was astonished. Her pale blue eyes filled with tears, and she began to sob as if her heart were broken.

Addie was mortified. "Nellie! Bad girl!"

"Guts!" Nellie shouted triumphantly.

"Ha!" Tilla roared with loud, rude, unqueenlike laughter. "She not fancy!"

"That's right. She's terrible. I'm afraid you will have to be thrown into the dungeon, Terrible Princess. Off you go to jail," Addie told Nellie. Addie jumped to her feet and tossed her squealing sister into the air. She tucked Nellie under her arm, then charged around and around the blanket. She dashed to the stream. Nellie laughed and laughed.

Tilla picked up tearful Katya, imitating Addie. "Katya flies, vooop! Right out da vindow."

"Into the jail!" Addie shouted. She and Tilla jumped over Rattling Creek with their sisters. Make-believe crowns tumbled. Nellie yowled with happiness. Katya squealed.

"This is what Miss Brophy should do to the Connolly boys. Lock them in jail and throw the key in the Jim River!" Addie said, twirling around with her sister one last time.

Tilla laughed and jumped back across the creek with Katya. "Good idea!"

"I know something better. Miss Brophy should just pitch both boys in the Jim," Addie said breathlessly. She rejoined Tilla and set her sister on the ground beside Katya. Now the little girls were sleepily rubbing their eyes.

"Maybe they're tired. Maybe we can get them to take a nap," Addie whispered.

Tilla nodded. She placed her sister on the blanket and folded one corner over her. Katya contentedly sucked her thumb, but Nellie was not so easily persuaded to sleep. She crawled about for a few more minutes, searching for crumbs of food. At last, she lay quietly on her stomach and began to snore.

The sun felt warm. Addie leaned back in the grass, staring up at the cloud shapes in the blue sky. Tilla did the same. It was very pleasant having a friend to visit, Addie thought. She was glad Mother had made gingermen, and she was glad she could share the gingermen with Tilla. This was a very special afternoon.

"Vat you see?" Tilla asked, squinting skyward and pointing at a cloud pushed hard by restless wind. "I see ship dat bring me here. After ship, ve come in vagon."

"You came to America on a ship?" asked Addie, whose family had made the trip to Dakota in a covered wagon. She had never considered other ways of traveling. "How long did it take?"

Tilla shrugged. "Da ship take many, many days. I forget. Everyone so sick. Da sea move up and down all da time. Up and down."

The journey in a ship sounded more uncomfortable than bumping along in a wagon, Addie thought. At least with a wagon a person could get out and walk.

"I not be sick. I da only one," Tilla rolled over on her stomach, resting her chin in her hands. "I stand on deck all da time. I like da sea. Sea look like dis place, moving up and down, up and down." Tilla gestured with her hands at the stretch of treeless prairie beyond their sheltered spot beside Rattling Creek. The grass was buffeted by the wind like waves.

Did the prairie really look like the sea? Addie wondered.

"You haf seen da sea?"

Addie shook her head.

"You haf seen mountains where snow on top all year?"

Addie shook her head. She had seen hills and bluffs near the Mississippi River when they lived in Iowa. But she had never seen mountains like the ones Miss Brophy talked about in geography, where no trees grew on the top and there was snow year-round.

"At home ve haf big mountains. Ve haf big trees. Ve haf trolls living in der."

"Trolls? What are trolls?"

Tilla laughed. "You not know trolls? My mudder know all about da trolls. She tell me. Trolls dey are tall, hairy and ugly, like dis." Tilla made a grotesque face. She stood up and stomped on the ground in a circle. "Vide, flat feet to valk on snow." She sniffed the air and put her hands to her ears. "Big nose. Big ears. Smell rabbits far away. Hear rabbits far away. Catch and gobble rabbits down."

"Has your mother ever seen a troll?"

"No. Not many sees trolls. Dey are magic."

41

Addie squinted at Tilla. Was she telling the truth? Or was this pretending, just like making believe that they were queens at a tea party? "Trolls don't sound too nice to me."

"Some are bad. Some are good. Good trolls find da lost child in da woods. Take da child home. Give him nice dinner — bowl of porridge, maybe. Maybe vit butter in middle. Dance for da child to cheer him up."

"And then what? Does the lost child have to stay with the trolls forever?"

Tilla sat down again. She hunched up with her knees nearly to her chin and chewed on a piece of grass. "Sometimes da child vant to stay. Never go home."

Never go home? That sounded terrible. What lost child would want to live with a big, hairy, ugly troll with huge feet and ears and nose? What child would never want to go home? Addie frowned. Norway must be a strange place.

"In Norvay you must be very, very careful not get lost," Tilla whispered. "Very, very careful."

Suddenly, from behind a cottonwood, a scary shape leapt toward them. Tilla and Addie screamed. "Aaaarrgggh! I am a troll!" the shape shouted. "I eat rabbits, and now I'm going to eat you, too!"

"George Sidney Mills! How dare you spy on us!" Addie said angrily.

George, who was wearing his shirt buttoned over his face

with peach willow branches sticking out of the neck, laughed and laughed.

Katya and Nellie woke up crying from all the noise. "Wait till I tell Mother on you," Addie shouted.

"Go ahead!" George said, swaggering just like the Connolly brothers. "See if I care."

Tilla sat her sobbing sister in her lap and stared accusingly at George. "You learning some mean tricks from dose Connolly boys. Dey no good. You should stay avay. Time for me and Katya go home now."

"Can't you stay a little longer?" Addie asked.

Tilla shook her head. "I told Mama I be back before sunset." Hurriedly, she handed Addie the map from her pocket. "Maybe someday you vill visit me. Den you need map." She gathered Katya in her arms. "Addie, tank you for da very nice time."

"You're welcome," Addie said half-heartedly. She was disappointed at the way the afternoon had ended.

Tilla started north, the way she had come.

George smiled. He was delighted Tilla and Katya were leaving. He had scared them away — that was something. Maybe he was getting as tough as the Connollys, the toughest boys in all of Hutchinson County.

"You'll never learn to read, George Sidney Mills!" Addie said angrily, using the most hurtful words she could think of. She wiped Nellie's tear-streaked, sticky face with a clean corner of her apron. "You'll never learn anything!"

"Don't care," George replied. His sister and Tilla acted like such goody-goodies all the time, and the teacher thought they were so wonderful. What did Miss Brophy know? Girls made him sick. He gave Addie his meanest scowl.

4 MISS TEACHER'S PET

The end of November drew near. The patchwork of bright colors on the prairie bleached and faded into pale yellow and soft brown. School was filled with interesting new discoveries for Addie. She learned how to multiply pesky numbers and what happened during the Revolutionary War and how to spell "Mississippi" so it sounded like a song. Even George was slowly but surely learning how to read.

On the days the Connolly boys were absent, the classroom was peaceful and the students worked diligently. But whenever Malcolm and Daniel appeared, chaos followed. A dead mouse would be discovered floating in the water bucket, or a clump of horse manure would be found on a bench. The Connolly boys just laughed and laughed. None of Miss Brophy's threats seemed to make any difference. They weren't scared, Addie decided, because Miss Brophy was too kind-hearted to give them the whipping they deserved.

Every day as Addie walked to school, she hoped the Connolly boys would be absent. Today, to cheer Miss Brophy, who was beginning to look strained from all the trouble with the bullies, Addie gathered a handful of deep purple-blue downy gentian — the last flower of the season — that she found near the old buffalo wallow.

"Why thank you, Addie! Thank you very much," Miss Brophy said when Addie gave her the fragile blossoms. She placed them in the jelly jar of water on her desk. "They remind me of the color of Lake Champlain, where I grew up in New York."

Lake Champlain and New York sounded very far away. Addie cleared her throat nervously. She hoped her teacher wasn't homesick. Because of the Connolly boys, Miss Brophy might be thinking of giving up teaching. What if she left Dakota forever?

"Here's something else, too," Addie said. She quickly handed Miss Brophy a poem she had written the night before on the back of one of Pa's mail-order catalog forms. It was titled "The Wild Prairie Rose." Addie had composed other poems since school had started, but this was the first she'd ever thought good enough to share. No one knew about the rest of her poems hidden under Ruby Lillian's mattress in the old cigar box.

Miss Brophy was the only person Addie had ever met

who loved poetry as much as she did. Miss Brophy knew all about rhyme and meter. In a lovely, melodious voice, she would recite from Henry Wadsworth Longfellow:

> *The day is done, and the darkness*
> *Falls on the wings of Night,*
> *As a feather is wafted downward*
> *From an eagle on his flight.*

Longfellow was Miss Brophy's favorite. Even his name sounded poetic.

"Addie, may I read it now?" Miss Brophy asked.

Addie took a deep breath and nodded. She wanted desperately for her teacher to like the poem. She longed for someone as fine as Miss Brophy to look at her and say, "Addie Mills, you are indeed special." She wanted Miss Brophy to think she was better than Donald Feeney and his perfect penmanship, better than Tilla Bergstrom and her quick grasp of English. Addie wanted Miss Brophy to like her the very best because she could do something no one — not even Donald or Tilla — could do. She could write a poem.

Miss Brophy was so absorbed in reading that she did not say anything when Malcolm Connolly and his brother Daniel climbed through the window and took their seats at the back of the room. The Connolly brothers talked and shouted in loud, rowdy voices. Miss Brophy did not pay any attention to the commotion.

All because of my poem, Addie thought, tipping back proudly on her heels.

Miss Brophy took off her glasses and smiled at Addie. "My, this is wonderful! You should be proud of yourself." Suddenly, she noticed Lorenzo Hebbert balanced on the windowsill, and she called, "Class! Class! I'd like you to take your seats. I have an announcement."

Addie felt so light-headed with her success that she nearly floated back to her bench. She was certain Miss Brophy intended to read her poem in front of all the children. What an honor!

"Boys and girls," Miss Brophy said, smoothing the crease of Addie's poem, "I'd like to tell you about something important."

Addie blushed. Miss Brophy considered her poem important. She hoped everyone else would, too, even though the horrible Connolly boys might laugh.

George wasn't interested in what the teacher had to say. Daniel and Malcolm Connolly had just taught him a song with real swear words in it, and he was enjoying singing it over and over under his breath, trying to make Addie furious. "Fifty miles from water, a hundred miles from wood, to hell with this damned country, I'm going home for good," he sang, then turned around and shouted hello to the Connollys.

Miss Brophy shot a warning glance in George's direction.

He faced the front of the room again but did not stop softly humming the awful song. "I'd like to announce," Miss Brophy continued, "that we will be having a special Christmas program in December. We are going to invite all of your families and neighbors for an oyster-stew supper here at our brand-new schoolhouse. Our class will provide the entertainment."

Addie sighed with disappointment. Miss Brophy was not going to read her poem aloud now. She was not going to announce, "Addie Mills is indeed special."

Malcolm belched loudly. "I know what I'll do that's sure entertaining. Anybody want to see me smash a couple of Rooshen heads together?"

Tommy Owens and Herbert Bradbury clapped and whistled approvingly. Although unable to understand English completely, the children from Russia seemed to sense that Malcolm was threatening them. Nervously, they moved closer together. Gunther turned and sneered an insult under his breath in German. Malcolm pelted him with small wads of paper.

"Malcolm! I would like you to come to the front of the classroom immediately and apologize to everyone for your interruption. I will not have this kind of disruptive, disgusting behavior here," Miss Brophy announced. Her face was flushed.

Malcolm sauntered up to the desk where Miss Brophy

was still seated. He towered over her in a leering, menacing fashion. "What are you going to do about it, Miss Teacher?" he demanded.

The children watched, breathless. Since school had begun, Malcolm's cruel bullying had become legendary. Everyone feared him, from five-year-old Rudolph Schuler to fourteen-year-old Conrad Shaver. Standing beside the desk, Malcolm appeared nearly twice as big as Miss Brophy and twice as powerful. The class did not belong to her. Today it belonged to him.

"Sit down at once and be quiet," she said icily, looking Malcolm straight in the eye. "Your parents will be hearing from me about your behavior."

"My pa don't care," Malcolm snorted. He put his hands in his pockets and strutted to his seat, unpunished and triumphant. He sat back with his immense muddy boots on his desk, enjoying the way everyone was looking at him.

Addie wished Miss Brophy would do something. Why didn't she try to stop him? Or was she afraid of Malcolm, too?

Miss Brophy's hand shook as she brushed a curl from her forehead. "For the Christmas program, you are all invited to either recite or sing a song. We want to demonstrate some of the things we have learned so far in class."

"I haven't learned anything," Daniel bellowed with pride. His brother slapped him on the back approvingly.

Miss Brophy ignored the comment and continued, her voice more high-pitched than usual. "For example, Addie Mills has submitted an original poem. I am going to encourage her to read this aloud to the parents. After her English lesson yesterday, Tilla and I talked about a lovely Christmas carol she's going to sing. Tilla is doing so well learning English that she may soon be assisting as a reading helper." Miss Brophy paused to smile at both girls. "I have several books of verse I will be happy to lend to anyone else who would like to recite."

"Show-off," George whispered.

Addie didn't hear a word her brother or anyone else said. She felt stunned. Her sometime friend had been invited to perform in the Christmas program first, before anyone else had even heard about it.

Addie thought about Tilla's private English lessons and all the extra attention she received from Miss Brophy. It wasn't fair. She turned to look at Tilla, who grinned with a big, warm, we're-in-this-together smile. Addie refused to smile back.

"Is something wrong, Addie?" Miss Brophy asked as she distributed paper for penmanship.

"No, ma'am," Addie replied, trying not to sound as disappointed as she felt.

"All right then. Let's begin today's penmanship lesson.

We will practice copying 'Better have no company than bad company.' For those of you using pens, please remember to put the tip of your forefinger flat upon the barrel of your pen holder, put the middle finger under the pen holder, and keep your arms and paper in line. I'd like you to copy this sentence fifteen times."

George groaned loudly, and someone laughed.

"Why do you enjoy acting like those troublemakers?" Addie hissed angrily at her brother. "I think the teacher picked that penmanship sentence just for you. 'Better have no company than bad company,' George."

"Why don't you mind your own business, Miss Teacher's Pet?" George growled. He tried to rub away a chalk smudge on the corner of his slate. His handwriting was so awkward that Miss Brophy had not yet allowed him to practice with a pen.

Miss Brophy motioned to Tilla, Fred Falkenberg, Donald Feeney, and Lorenzo and Lucia Hebbert. Ever since the McGuffey Readers had finally arrived, Addie had assisted this small group. Until today, being Miss Brophy's reading assistant made Addie feel grown-up and helpful. Would she feel so special when Tilla was doing the same job?

"I'd like you to practice Lesson Twelve. Addie will read aloud, and then each of you will have a turn to repeat the passage," Miss Brophy said.

Donald Feeney passed out the books. Tilla took the seat next to Addie and listened carefully as she read Lesson Twelve aloud:

>*Clink, clink, clinkerty, clink!*
>*We begin to hammer at morning's blink,*
>*And hammer away*
>*Till the busy day,*
>*Like us, aweary, to rest shall sink.*
>
>*Clink, clink, clinkerty, clink!*
>*From labor and care we never will shrink,*
>*But our fires we'll blow*
>*Till our forges glow*
>*With light intense, while our eyelids wink.*

Addie looked over her shoulder when she finished, hoping to find that Miss Brophy was listening approvingly. Instead, she saw George across the room making nasty faces at her. Silently, he mouthed "clink, clink, clinkerty, clink" and hit himself on the top of the head with an invisible hammer.

"Please can you tell vat means da vord here *labor?*" Tilla asked, pointing to the text.

"Labor. Labor. Let me think a minute," Addie mumbled. She didn't want Tilla to know she wasn't sure. Miss Brophy's special reading helper was supposed to know everything.

"Doesn't it mean 'work'? You know, work, work, work," Fred said, standing up and demonstrating how to shovel so that Tilla would understand the new English word.

She appeared more confused.

"Maybe *labor* means a job. What people do all day. Maybe like service," Lorenzo suggested helpfully.

"Service!" Tilla said, her face brightening. "I know about dat. My sisters all in service. Dey go to town. Den dey clean, cook for da people der. Den dey give all da money to Papa for da family."

"Your sisters are maids?" Donald asked with the slightest hint of disgust.

"No. Not maids. Dey in service," Tilla said proudly. "Let me read dis now."

Addie handed the book to Tilla, who struggled fiercely with the English and refused to give up until she successfully reached the poem's end, "vile our eyelids vink."

From the corner of her eye, Addie saw Miss Brophy smile fondly at her pupil from Norway. Tilla could hardly speak English when she walked into the classroom. Now she was reading aloud without help from anyone. It was annoying.

Addie made a silent vow. She might have shared picnics and gingermen and make-believe with Tilla, but she would never share Ruby Lillian with her. Absolutely never.

5 REVENGE

At lunchtime, Addie sat on the sunny side of the schoolhouse, out of the biting wind. The children from Russia relaxed a few feet away, laughing and talking together, eating odd-shaped dumplings and cold sausages they had brought to school wrapped in handkerchief bundles.

"I sit vit you?" Tilla asked.

"Did you forget your lunch again?" Addie sighed, remembering another reason why Tilla annoyed her. She always ate half of Addie's lunch. Reluctantly, Addie unwrapped her butter sandwich and tore off a piece for Tilla, who had not brought a lunch pail since school began.

"Ya, I vas in a big hurry," Tilla replied. She gobbled the bread. Addie wondered if the Norwegian girl ever ate breakfast. She always seemed so hungry by noon.

"*Takk for maten.* I mean, tank you. Dis is very good.

My mudder is a very good cook. In my Old Country she cook for da king."

Addie chewed slowly, with her mouth politely closed, and watched Tilla rudely lick every last bit of butter from between her fingers. The day before she had told Addie about *nisser,* little magic men with wooden shoes and tall, pointed, red caps who protected her family's farm from harm. Back in Norway, Tilla had bragged, she used to visit a certain waterfall on three successive Thursday nights. When she threw food into the water, invisible creatures in the river played beautiful music. Even more incredible were Tilla's tales of horrible underground monsters who stole babies before they were christened. The monsters had to be frightened away with steel and fire.

Creatures who played beautiful music? Monsters who stole babies? Steel and fire? Trolls with big feet and ears? Addie could hardly believe a word of what Tilla said anymore. And when Tilla wasn't trying to scare Addie with her mother's old Norwegian tales, she was boasting about everyone in her family. She claimed her father was fabulously rich. She said her uncle, who lived next door, had a thousand cows and two thousand pigs.

And now, with a perfectly serious face, Tilla was telling Addie that her mother was once the Norwegian king's cook. Whoever heard of so many fantastic lies? "If your mother's such a wonderful cook, why doesn't she ever make lunch for you?" Addie demanded.

"She busy singing. You don't tink I say da troot?" Tilla lifted her chin in stubborn defiance. "I tell troot. Ven my broder come, ask him. He strong as ten men."

"All right. All right. I believe you," Addie said with another sigh, wondering if it was better to eat lunch alone or with a braggart who didn't know the difference between reality and make-believe. "The king's cook must have a very impressive house," Addie said, hoping to trick Tilla. "What does your house look like?"

Tilla was very quiet as she followed the trail of an ant with a piece of grass. "My house is big and vite. Much bigger even den big vite schoolhouse."

"Bigger than our schoolhouse?" Addie replied, carefully unwrapping a piece of cheese so that Tilla would not see it. This was a treat she wanted all to herself.

"Can I taste?" Tilla asked. "I love goat cheese."

"It's not goat cheese. Whoever heard of goat cheese? It's from a cow, and my mother made it. Here, take some if you're still starving to death."

The thin girl chewed noisily. She looked as if she were enjoying Addie's cheese very much.

"It's good, isn't it?"

"Everyting in America is good. I tell dis to my mudder.

She not listen. She say, 'Alvays strangers here. Ve never be Americans.' "

"Why does she say that?"

"She vant to go home, back to Trondelag and da mountains. She lonely. She cry all da time some days."

Addie recalled how homesick and sad Mother had been when they came to Dakota. Addie's most disturbing memory of that journey was for the first time seeing her mother cry. What if Mother had never grown accustomed to their new life here? What if she had never stopped weeping and longing for relatives and friends left behind?

Addie wondered what she would do if she were Tilla. "Does your mother speak English? Maybe that would be a good start."

Tilla shook her head. "I say, 'Learn English!' But she speak *Norsk* only." She dropped the last crumb of cheese into her mouth. "Ve play crack da vip now?"

Addie couldn't help smiling at Tilla's pronunciation of her favorite game, crack the whip. "Yes, but we'll need to find some others to play with us. And I have to check on George first. I told my mother I would keep my eye on him." She stood up and looked around the schoolyard. Mother was worried about George's behavior. It did not seem fair to Addie, however, that she was the one who had to keep track of her bad brother.

There was George crawling under the schoolhouse, hurriedly stuffing small pebbles into his pockets.

Addie hurried closer. "What are you doing?" she demanded.

"Nothing," George said, and grinned mischievously.

"I know what you're doing. You're collecting rocks. Why?"

"No reason."

"Georg-ie! You finished?" Malcolm shouted, loping across the schoolyard with his brother, Tommy Owens, and Herbert Bradbury. The three boys followed Malcolm everywhere.

George hissed nervously at his sister. "Why don't you leave me alone? Can't you see I'm busy?"

Undaunted, Addie turned to the biggest Connolly boy. "Why are you telling my brother to collect rocks? What are you going to do with them?"

"Eat them for lunch, Miss Teacher's Pet, what do you think?" Malcolm laughed. His friends elbowed each other hard and chuckled. "Come on, Georgie. Give them to me."

Obediently, George poured the rocks into Malcolm's broad palms. Daniel flipped a rock in the air and caught it, then twirled around and shot it at the group of children still eating their lunch. Lena, the littlest girl from Russia, screamed and began crying.

"Oh, be quiet over there! Only babies cry," Daniel called.

"Not now, Gopher Brains," Malcolm sneered. He hooked

his thumbs in his dirty overall straps. "I said later, after school. Then we get them for sure."

Addie watched the boys saunter toward the other side of the schoolhouse. She grabbed George's arm.

"Don't go. You aren't going to throw rocks at the Rooshens, are you? Somebody might get hurt. And then you'll really be in trouble."

George only gave her a sheepish look and wriggled free. He started after Malcolm.

"You better not, George Sidney Mills. You'll get punished," Addie called.

George turned. For the first time, his face revealed fear. But he shrugged defiantly at his sister and kept walking.

"Vat dey doing?" Tilla asked.

"I think they're going to stone the Rooshens after school." The Norwegian girl looked confused.

"You know, throw rocks at them," Addie explained, motioning with her arms.

"Rocks," Tilla murmured. "Ve better tell da teacher."

Addie knew Tilla was right. She had to let Miss Brophy know of Malcolm's plan. Yet how could she? Telling the teacher would mean punishment for her brother. It would also mean enduring Malcolm's revenge.

"Miss Brophy!" Tilla called to their teacher, who was about to ring the bell for everyone to go back inside again.

"What is it, Tilla?"

"Tell her," Tilla said, pushing Addie in front of her.

"Miss Brophy, after school today Malcolm and Daniel are going to throw rocks at the Rooshens. We heard them say so," Addie blurted out all in one breath. "They already hit Lena over there."

Miss Brophy rushed over to the group of children huddled around the littlest Russian, who was still sobbing. She examined Lena's arm, then wiped her tears with her handkerchief. Taking the little girl by the hand, Miss Brophy led her inside the schoolhouse. "Tilla," she said quietly before she closed the door, "would you mind ringing the bell? I have something important to see to." Miss Brophy's dark eyes had a flash of fierce determination that Addie had never seen before.

Tilla rang the bell, and the children came inside and took their seats. All the windows except one had been shut.

"I see that, as usual, the Connolly boys are tardy," Miss Brophy said. "Since they seem to prefer entering class by the window, will you please shut the door for me, Donald?"

Donald closed the door.

Miss Brophy stood by the open window, holding something behind her back.

The children watched in suspense. Daniel's and Malcolm's hands and then their heads appeared in the window. The boys pulled themselves slowly inside, unaware that Miss Brophy was waiting.

CRACK! *CRACK!* The peach willow switch landed hard on their backs, heads, and hands. Addie flinched as the Connolly boys tumbled through the window and landed in a heap. Miss Brophy hit Malcolm and Daniel again. The Connollys crouched against the floor, shrunken. They bent over and hugged their arms to shield themselves from more blows. Finally Daniel and Malcolm stumbled out the door, whimpering. Miss Brophy did not stop them.

"Now all those with stones in their pockets can empty them on my desk immediately," Miss Brophy said, her voice shaking. She seemed to be trying to catch her breath. "Don't be shy. I know who you are. If you do not bring the stones forward, you will find yourself switched just as severely."

George, Tommy, and Herbert reluctantly trudged to the front of the classroom and dumped out the contents of their pockets. The stones clattered across Miss Brophy's desk.

The three boys were ordered to stand in a corner for the rest of the day. "And that is the end of that. We will have no more disruptions in my class," Miss Brophy said firmly. And for the first time since school began, Addie was hopeful she might be right.

As soon as class was dismissed, George stalked home by himself. Addie would have to walk home alone. She lingered to help stack the readers on the shelf. Tilla was waiting for her English lesson, but Miss Brophy put on her hat and coat.

"Tilla, I must go to town to tell the school board supervisor what happened today," Miss Brophy said. "Perhaps Addie will keep you company for a few minutes until your brother comes with the wagon."

Miss Brophy closed the door and waved goodbye to the girls, who walked to the clearing beyond the empty schoolyard. This was where Tilla waited every day for her brother to come.

The sky was almost dark. A cold wind blew. Suddenly, out from some tall grass sprang Malcolm and Daniel. "Well, hello, Miss Teacher's Pet," said Malcolm. The welts from the whipping still showed on his face and neck. As he circled around and around Addie, he flipped a large rock back and forth between his hands. "We know you're the one who told the teacher about our plan to get the dirty Rooshens. You think you can get away with that?"

Daniel grabbed Addie tightly by her arm. She tried to wrench free. "What'll it be, Malcolm?" Daniel said, his grip tightening. "Should we break one or both arms?"

Malcolm laughed. Addie stood motionless, unable even to scream. Miss Brophy was gone, and the schoolhouse was locked. She knew she couldn't run away or defend herself. *They were going to break her arms.*

63

"I didn't do it," Addie blurted.

"Didn't do what?" Daniel jeered, twisting Addie's arm hard.

"I didn't tell the teacher," Addie said between clenched teeth. "Tilla did."

All the color drained from Tilla's face. She slowly backed away.

"This little Norsky?"

Addie nodded. Malcolm loosened his grip, and she ran out of reach.

"Hey, you Norsky! We got some words with you!" Daniel and his brother shouted, stooping to pick up a few more rocks.

Addie's heart sank. Why did she say it? Now they'd hurt Tilla.

"Go avay. You smell bad, America boy."

Addie could hardly believe her eyes. The Norwegian girl came barely to the big boy's shoulder, and there she was, roaring with loud, disrespectful laughter and spitting right in his face! *"Pokkers ta deg!"* she hissed, using a phrase Addie knew was one of Tilla's favorites. In English it meant "The devil take you!"

Slowly, Malcolm wiped his eyes with his shirt. "You shouldn't have done that, Norsky."

"Ya? I'm not fearing you," she taunted, and bounded

quickly away. Malcolm and Daniel tried to catch her, but they were not fast enough. She ran like the wind, darting back and forth across the road to where her brother and the wagon always came.

Addie was tempted to run home while the Connollys chased Tilla. But she knew she couldn't leave. Tilla was incredibly brave, incredibly foolish. There was no one except Addie to help her — at least, until Tilla's brother came.

Anxiously, Addie scanned the empty road. Where is he? Please, God, bring Tilla's brother, she prayed. Bring him now.

"Get her!" Malcolm shouted.

"Leave her alone!" Addie screamed.

The Connolly boys paid no attention to Addie. They had a new victim now. Addie searched the road again. A quarter of a mile away, she saw a shape approaching. Tilla must have seen it, too. It was a good thing she was keeping the Connolly boys so busy trying to catch her. They did not have a chance to notice the horse and wagon.

Addie raced to meet Tilla's brother. "Hurry! We need help!" she screamed. "Tilla is in terrible trouble!"

The enormous young man with broad shoulders, muscular arms, flaxen hair, and a missing front tooth pulled the horse to a halt. Without speaking a word, he leapt from the wagon. In spite of his huge size, he ran nimbly all the way to the clearing.

"Ole! Ole!" Tilla yelled.

Like a turkey buzzard swooping after a pair of jack rabbits, Ole grabbed Malcolm and Daniel by the straps of their overalls and lifted them into the air, where he allowed them to struggle for several moments. The two wriggling boys appeared weightless as Tilla's brother, forearms bulging, brought them crashing together. They writhed in terror, begging for mercy. Ole only growled something Addie couldn't understand.

"Put us down!" Malcolm sobbed. "We didn't mean nothing. We weren't going to hurt her."

Tilla shouted a warning to her brother. Addie guessed she was cautioning him not to kill them.

Ole looked closely at his bruised victims and dropped them in the dirt. Stunned, Malcolm and Daniel wobbled away into the tall grass as quickly as they could.

Ole did not even look at them. He mumbled a command to his sister and motioned to the wagon. It was time to go home.

"Goodbye! Goodbye, Tilla! Goodbye, Ole!" Addie called weakly as the wagon disappeared down the road toward Ree Heights. For the first time, Tilla did not seem like such a tremendous liar. Her brother was every bit as strong as ten men, just as she had said. "Goodbye! Thank you!" Addie shouted.

Neither Tilla nor her brother turned around.

6   THE PRONGHORN
ANTELOPE

Before supper that evening, the first real blizzard of the season roared across Hutchinson County. For the next two days, yammering wind pounded the Millses' little soddy with sharp white flakes and cold that cut like steel into skin. It was the worst winter weather he'd ever seen, Pa said — "a regular blue whistler." He laughed, trying to cheer Mother, who worried the roof might blow away. "Now I know why those Dakota land agents don't tell the truth," Pa said cheerfully. "Nobody'd believe them."

The morning after the storm, everything was strangely still and dark as night. To conserve kerosene, Mother lit a rag in a dish of fat. The shaken sod overhead had sifted a fine layer of grime on everything, including the sleeping children's faces. Addie stared uncertainly at the ceiling. Would it hold?

The one-room soddy was just fourteen by eighteen feet wide, and it was crowded with mattresses and bedding. For two long, cold days, Addie and her brothers and sister had stayed in bed, dressed in shoes and coats to keep warm. The trundle bed, which tucked under their parents' bed, was shared by George and his two brothers. Addie and Nellie May slept on a feather tick on the floor. Ordinarily at daybreak, all the bedding was folded and stored inside a trunk, which also served as a place to sit. Not today. The children waited under their covers, wondering when they could climb out of their beds at last.

Addie sat up, shivering. She pulled the blanket around her shoulders. At least the wind did not blow through the cracks in the walls as fiercely as it had last winter. Pa had covered the inside walls with several layers of newspaper. Addie watched him inspect the ceiling. The roof, he said, was in no danger of collapsing. That was some relief. But the drifts around the house were so deep that he was barely able to shove open the door and poke a hole to daylight with a broom handle.

After a long time, Pa managed to clear away the snow from the doorway and window. The children were able to see for themselves that the sky was clear, and the sun shone as bright as in July. George, Lew, and Burt were so excited they jumped out of bed and cheered. "The storm is over!

The storm is over!" Lew shouted. He did a little dance with Nellie May, who squealed with delight.

The boys helped Addie put away the bedding. Unlike her brothers and sister, Addie knew that it was still too cold to escape the soddy, no matter how bright the sun. She had already seen one Dakota winter come and go. No warmth radiated from this kind of winter sky.

"Mother, can we go out now?" begged George. He was tired of being cooped up inside. He longed to run and shout and leap and play fox-and-geese in the snow.

"Absolutely not. It's much too cold. And I don't think you'd fancy frostbite," Mother warned. She tossed another armful of hay cats into the stove. "The last time Pa checked the thermometer, the mercury had gone down into the ball. It might be thirty below zero."

George pouted.

The family quickly finished a small meal of porridge made by boiling snow water and corn meal. Pa went back outside to tend the animals. As soon as the dishes were washed in a bucket of melted snow, Mother sat down and began sewing patches on the boys' pants. Addie climbed up into her favorite place, a wide ledge under the soddy's only window. When Pa and their neighbor, Mr. Fency, had built the house a year ago, they had used two-foot-thick sod bricks. The gap for the wooden window frame was fitted with a pane of costly glass that had come all the way from the East.

If she were careful to hunch her head and shoulders and keep her knees bent, the window ledge was just big enough for Addie — and no one else. In a house filled with a mother, father, three noisy brothers, and a bothersome, toddling sister, this was the only place Addie could go for the least bit of privacy. The problem was, of course, that George, Lew, Burt, and even Nellie May wanted to sit in the window ledge, too, and they all had to take turns.

Addie started to make a picture by chipping frost from the glass with her fingernail. But somehow she couldn't concentrate on what she was doing. She peered out at the new, dazzling white, cold landscape and thought about how the Connollys had tried to hurt Tilla.

For the past two days, Addie had longed to reach out across the snowdrifts, all the way to Tilla's big white house at Ree Heights and tell her she was sorry. Over and over in her mind she saw Tilla, frightened and skinny, darting here and there in the clearing like a prairie dog with a hawk circling overhead. Addie knew she had been a coward and a liar. Maybe she didn't deserve to be forgiven. If Ole hadn't come along when he did, Daniel and Malcolm might have hurt Tilla badly! And it would all have been Addie's fault. Guilt gnawed at her insides. There was nobody to tell. Even George would be disgusted. And she could never talk to

Mother or Pa about what happened. She was too ashamed.

How could she say she was sorry? Even though she had saved the map showing the route to Tilla's house, most landmarks would have disappeared in the drifting snow. And the bitter cold would prevent anyone from traveling far, anyway. She would have to wait until school started again to see Tilla and apologize. It was hard to say which was worse, the endless waiting or finally facing Tilla in person.

Addie squinted outside through the sun's glare. She wondered what the schoolhouse must look like now. Smothered in snow, the prairie beyond her family's soddy stretched farther than ever. Blue sky hung like a long curtain at the edge of the world. Nothing looked familiar. The sea of dancing prairie grass was gone. The place beside Rattling Creek where she and Ruby Lillian played school had disappeared, too. A great white mountain stood where there were once chokecherry bushes. The best hide-and-seek hollows were filled in, level as tables. And the day before the blizzard struck, the weather had been so sunny and fine!

Addie saw that drifts had buried the clothesline with two of George's shirts and a pair of Pa's trousers on it. There had been no time to think of bringing in the laundry. The blizzard came up so suddenly that Pa and George were barely able to herd Big Jones and the two other cows inside the sod barn. Then they had pulled themselves into the house using the rope Pa had strung up earlier in case of just such an emergency.

She listened to the sound of Pa shoveling a narrow path from the house to the barn. He needed to break the ice in the water trough, feed the hungry cows, pigs, and chickens, and do the milking. The storm was so bad yesterday that it had not been safe to venture outside, even holding on to the rope. The scritch-scritcha-scritch-scrape of Pa's shovel biting the snow and ice was comforting, like the sound a pan of bread made sliding across the oven rack. His shoveling meant the storm was finally over. The family would soon be dug out. They were still together, safe and sound.

"Addie, want to hear a funny story Malcolm told me?" George asked.

"I am not interested in the least in what no-good Malcolm told you," she replied, positioning her feet squarely so that her brother could not pull her down from the ledge, the way he often did.

"I'll tell you, anyway," George said, grinning. "There was this man, see? He lived out near Larimore. It was so cold when he died, they just sharpened his feet and drove him into the ground. Ha-ha-ha!" George slapped his leg just like Malcolm Connolly.

Addie winced.

"Bet the blizzard buried the school," George said happily.

"If we're lucky, maybe the place caved in." He jumped to look out the window over Addie's knees. "I guess we won't have to go this week after all."

"Guess you don't know much. Didn't you hear Pa say he'd take us in the sleigh?" Addie said, pushing her brother away from the ledge with her foot. Suddenly, she had a terrible thought. When they returned to school, what if Tilla refused to forgive her?

"When are you going to get down? It's my turn," George demanded, interrupting her thoughts.

"Just a minute. I'm nearly finished." In the window frost, she scratched the final touches on a picture of a boy with crossed eyes and ugly horns. She tried to drive from her mind the awful image of Tilla refusing to forgive her. Instead, she thought about something pleasant: Annabelle. Addie had never stopped hoping that this perfect friend would one day appear. Maybe when school started again, Annabelle would arrive, just settled in Dakota from Michigan or Illinois or Iowa. Addie would be helpful and friendly, showing her gentle, pretty friend where to hang her coat. Perhaps at lunch they would trade sandwiches and tell secrets.

"Who's that you're drawing?" George asked suspiciously.

"You'll never guess, George Sidney Mills. Never in a million years," Addie replied, adding the initials GSM.

"Scratch that picture off this minute or I'm telling."

"You two stop arguing. You'll wake Nellie May," Mother said. She was pouring a shallow bowl of sudsy water so Lew and Burt could make their own snow with one of Pa's old pipes. The little boys sat happily under the table, taking turns blowing bubbles. "Addie, go down in the root cellar and get some corn for George to shell. I need to start soaking the kernels for tomorrow's hominy."

George gave Addie a murderous look. He didn't like scraping kernels using the sharp metal corn sheller that sometimes blistered and cut his fingers. When her mother wasn't looking, Addie stuck out her tongue at her brother. Then she opened the trap door in the floor and stepped down a short ladder into the root cellar.

The cellar was dark and smelled of onions that hung in bunches. Addie had to be careful not to bump her head on the rafters, where smoked bacon hung. She gathered an armful of dried ears of corn from a barrel. Nearby stood row upon row of tomatoes Mother had canned in jars. There were barrels of potatoes and carrots buried in dirt so that they would not freeze and turn black. In several crocks were cucumbers and sliced cabbages pickled in vinegar and slabs of pork and beef preserved in brine. Greased eggs were hidden in a barrel of grain.

"George would be happy to help shell corn, Mother," Addie replied sweetly as she climbed out of the cellar and handed her brother the corn. She shut the trap door and went back to work in the window ledge, chiseling a long tail for the frost boy on the glass. Suddenly, she stopped.

Six black, magical eyes were clearly staring at her out near the drifts covering the creek. Were they escaped cows? Addie peered closer and saw the tawny and white shapes ruffle in the wind like an old barn owl rearranging its feathers. They certainly did not look like cows, unless the snow's glare was playing tricks on her eyes.

"Look at that!" she whispered.

"What?" George replied.

"I think they're pronghorn antelope."

"Move over and let me see."

Addie climbed off the ledge so George could have a better view.

"They must be starving in this deep snow," George said. He whistled quietly. This was the closest the children had ever been to the elegant, long-legged creatures. Last winter, a small group had come to visit their homestead, lingering in a nearby field. George and Addie had spotted them from the creek. George was convinced the antelope were attracted to his bright wool scarf. He seemed to fancy he could have spoken to them, if only they had come closer. "Antelope language," George had said, "sounds a little like Rooshen talk — only softer, with some tongue-clicking noises in there."

Addie knew George had only wished he could understand antelope talk. The animals hadn't come to speak to him. They'd come to nibble the few crippled cornstalks still in the field. Pa said there were only a handful of pronghorns left in this part of Dakota. The rest had been hunted down, just like the herds of buffalo that disappeared before the Mills family had come to homestead.

Maybe these pronghorns outside their window were all that were left — the last three survivors in all of Hutchinson County.

"You know how fast antelope run? They're the fastest things alive," George said softly. "Pa told me he once saw one running out near the dried-up lake bed, nearly flat to the ground, racing faster than anything just for the enjoyment of it."

"Faster even than a steam locomotive?"

George nodded. "Just think what it must have been like when a whole herd stampeded."

"I wish I could have seen that," Addie said.

George had a faraway look in his eye. "Maybe I could go away with them," he whispered to no one in particular. "Maybe I could be their friend."

The children stared at the three pronghorns for a long time without speaking. Addie wondered what it must be like to be hungry and caught in deep snow with nothing to eat and nowhere to go. Why didn't Pa's shoveling scare the antelope away? The animals must plainly see that this was a house, with people inside and smoke coming from the smokestack. They seemed so unafraid. It must be hunger that made them so reckless.

"Perhaps the antelope would like a pan of scraps. Maybe a few crusts of bread or some leftover porridge or a handful of dry corn. Mother might not mind," Addie said.

Just as she turned from the window to ask, it happened.

An explosion split the quiet. One of the antelopes crumpled into the snow. Two, three more rifle shots brought down the others. The children stared, their mouths open in disbelief. Nellie May woke up, screaming.

"What's going on out there? Where's Pa? Can you see Pa?" Mother demanded, rushing to the window, her face filled with terror. Lew and Burt ran over and hid their faces in her skirt. Speechless, Addie and George watched as a pair of bundled shapes in long snowshoes appeared. They shuffled across the snow toward the fallen animals.

"Now I see Pa. He's all right," George said hoarsely. "It's hunters. They just shot our antelope."

Sadness weighed upon Addie's shoulders like a heavy load. If I hadn't looked away, would the pronghorn still be alive? she wondered. I could have warned them if I'd seen the hunters coming. I could have saved them.

They were most likely the last in all Hutchinson County. She might never see antelope again.

The hunters were struggling through the deep snow to haul the animals away. It took two men to drag one antelope. She turned from the window, unable to watch anymore.

"What do those men with guns think they're doing, shooting on our property, scaring us to death?" Mother said under her breath. "Can you make out who they are?"

"No, I can't," George replied bitterly. His face was flushed and his eyes squinted with anger. "Those pronghorn weren't bothering nobody. Why'd they have to die?"

7 RATTLESNAKES AND PEPPERMINTS

A blast of cold air filled the soddy. Towering in the doorway was a snow-covered shape. His beard and the scarf wrapped around his neck were frozen stiff and white. The door swung shut.

"Put on the coffee pot, Becca. I'm nearly frozen to death," Pa said in a tired voice. He winked at Addie, then threw her his snowy muskrat cap. She gave it a good shake and hung it on its peg. Even though his moustache was encrusted with ice, Addie could see Pa's mouth was a hard little line. He slumped into a chair near the stove.

"Samuel, what happened out there just now? Who were those hunters?" Mother demanded, pouring Pa a mug of coffee.

Pa sighed. "I tried talking to them. They've taken two of the antelope and will be back for the third. Couldn't understand a word they said. They were Norwegians, I think."

Norwegians, Addie thought grimly. It was Tilla's people

who had trespassed and killed the last of the pronghorns. She suddenly felt angry at Tilla, as if Tilla had personally taken part in what happened out there.

"Why'd they have to go and shoot the pronghorn?" George demanded. "Pa, didn't you say they might be the last?"

Pa nodded slowly, cradling the steaming mug in his hands. "So few have been sighted this past year, I suspect those antelope were the last we'll ever see in Hutchinson County. Of course, the hunters didn't know that. I've heard tell that this newest group of Norwegians is pretty bad off — they don't have enough cash to buy supplies and they didn't have enough time to put in a crop. It's going to be a long, hungry winter for them. I'm letting the men take the meat home for their families."

"But it's our land, Pa," Addie said angrily. "Couldn't they see our house? Couldn't they see somebody living here? Don't they know you can't go shooting on other people's property?"

"What's done is done. Not everybody in Dakota's fortunate enough to have had a good harvest," Pa replied. "Not everybody's lucky enough to have a strong house built, and enough food set by. We're doing all right. But there are others who aren't. Bad luck and hunger can make a man desperate. Addie, if you and your brothers and sister were hungry, I'd have shot those antelope myself."

Addie stared hard at her father, unable to imagine him shooting anything as precious as the last antelope. But his words about bad luck echoed in her head. She thought about how hungry Tilla always was. If Tilla's mother was such a wonderful cook, why didn't Tilla ever come to school with a lunch pail? Why did she always take half of Addie's food? After listening to Tilla's exaggerated stories, it was difficult to know what was true and what was make-believe. What if Tilla's people were the ones who were starving?

"Somebody's coming!" Lew shouted from the window.

There was a loud rapping. Pa pulled open the door and a tall man in a furry hat stepped inside. "Sorry to bother you folks," he said. "But I've got a sick cow I'm in need of help with. It's Old No Horn. I can't afford to lose her. Samuel, can you come?"

"Step inside and make yourself warm, Mr. Fency. You must be nearly frozen," Mother replied, pulling a chair close to the stove. "Let me give you some hot coffee."

Their friend and neighbor took up a lot of room in the little soddy, even when he took off his big beaver hat and sat down. "Looks like somebody's been doing some hunting on your property," Mr. Fency said.

"Norwegians," Pa replied quietly. "They'll be back later for the other antelope."

"Hope they've got more than just antelope to eat until

spring," Mr. Fency said. He rubbed the frost from his beard, smiled at the children, and drummed his long fingers on his bony knee. Nellie May laughed and toddled close.

"What do you got in your pockets this time, Mr. Fency?" Burt demanded with an expectant grin. It was a game they played whenever they saw each other.

"Don't be so rude, Burton Grant. Polite people don't ask questions like that," Mother scolded.

"Rattlesnakes. Massasauga rattlesnakes," Mr. Fency said mysteriously. "I keep them in my pockets on cold days like this."

Lew and Burt shrieked with delight. "And what do you feed the rattlers, Mr. Fency?" Burt asked slyly.

"Why, in summertime I feed them great hundred-pound sweet potatoes because they have such enormous appetites. But in wintertime," he paused and winked, "I feed them peppermints because they're slow and sluggish, and they can hold those peppermints in their mouths all day and sleep at the same time."

"Are they sleeping now?" Burt whispered.

"I believe so," Mr. Fency replied. "I suppose I might be able, if I'm very careful not to disturb the rattlesnakes, to give you a few of the extra peppermints. Would you like that?"

"Yes! Yes!" the little boys replied excitedly. Even Nellie

May seemed to understand that something wonderful was about to happen. She clapped her pudgy hands together.

Wincing, as if at any moment he might be bitten, Mr. Fency shut his eyes tight. Slowly, carefully, he slipped his hand into his pocket. Burt and Lew held their breath. Mr. Fency pressed a perfect white oval peppermint into each of the children's hands.

"What do you say?" Mother said, smiling.

"Thank you, snakes!" Burt and Lew shouted.

Addie had to hold Nellie May's candy and let her lick so she wouldn't choke. After she lost interest, the sticky-faced baby crawled under the table to untie Mr. Fency's bootlaces. When no one was looking, Addie popped Nellie May's peppermint into her own mouth so it wouldn't go to waste.

"How is dear Anna?" Mother asked. "We haven't visited in so long. I hope she's well."

"Fit as a fiddle," Mr. Fency said. "She sends her love. We haven't seen you children since school started. How is school, Addie?"

"School's fine," Addie said, her face beaming. "My teacher's name is Miss Brophy, and I like her."

George didn't say anything. He sat scowling on the window seat.

"I heard she's boarding with the Madson family this term.

George Madson told me she plans to homestead a claim all by herself. She's got about 160 acres."

"You don't say!" Pa replied.

"Addie talks about her teacher all the time. I haven't had a chance to meet Miss Brophy yet," Mother said. "You know, Mr. Fency, we just found out that Addie's going to recite her very own poem at the school program. Isn't that wonderful news? Maybe you and Anna would like to come along and see her. And see George, too, of course."

"I'd like that. I know Anna would, too," Mr. Fency said and smiled. "Addie, I'm proud of you. Just think, you're a real poet."

George made a face at his sister. Addie blushed.

"George Madson says the new teacher's not much bigger than some of the boys she's had to horsewhip in her class," Mr. Fency continued. "While I was in Scotland two days ago I heard that Bill Connolly's two boys aren't going back to school. Seems she gave them a memorable licking."

Addie glanced triumphantly at her brother. The bullies were gone forever!

George frowned. Was Mr. Fency telling the truth? If so, this was the worst news he'd heard since Mother announced he had to go to school in the first place. What would it be like every day in that boring classroom without Daniel and Malcolm to liven things up? Like prison, that's what.

"Can't say that I blame their teacher. From what I've heard, those Connolly boys are bad as they come." Mr. Fency stood up and pulled on his coat.

"We'd better get going," Pa said. "I'll need to finish feeding my own cattle before we go back to your place. Becca, I hope to be back before nightfall."

"Goodbye, and thank you for the coffee," Mr. Fency said.

"Take this for Anna," Mother said, hurriedly rolling a bundle of fabric scraps. including the turkey-red calico left over from Addie's school apron and George's shirt. "I don't know when I'll see her again. And I know she can always use some new quilting pieces."

"Can I come, Pa?" George asked. So many emotions churned inside him, he felt as though he might burst. He just had to escape the cramped house.

"You stay here and help your mother," Pa replied. The soddy door slammed shut.

8 "WHEN I GROW UP..."

Mother gave the coffee mugs to Addie to rinse and handed an armful of corncobs, a wooden bowl, and the scraper to George. He lowered himself slowly from the window seat and leaned against the wall. "You feeling all right, George?" Mother asked. "You're awfully quiet."

George turned away. Why couldn't everybody leave him alone?

"It's too bad about what happened to the antelope," Mother continued. She held her hand gently against George's face to see if he might have a fever.

He wriggled angrily away and reached for the root cellar trap door. "I'm all right," George replied gruffly. "This isn't near enough corn. I'm going down for more."

Addie was relieved that George was out of the way. She sat down at the table and watched her mother lift bread dough from a bowl and set it on a floured breadboard. She punched and turned the dough again and again.

Mother's sleeves were pushed up past her red, worn elbows. The smear of flour on her cheek was nearly the same color as the streak of white in her hair. She handed Addie a piece of dough. While Addie kneaded, she noticed for the first time that her mother's everyday black dress was frayed around the cuffs.

Mother wasn't anything like Miss Brophy, Addie decided. Miss Brophy never came to school in old clothes. Her dresses were pretty and new, her hair was always neatly combed, and she always smelled like rosewater. Mother did not smell like rosewater — she smelled like flour. And the skin on her hands was calloused and dry and covered with blue veins and splotches. Mother even had little wrinkles around her mouth and eyes. What if Tilla had been lying? Maybe Mother wasn't beautiful. Maybe she was just old and plain.

Mother did not know anything about poetry, either. Why, just yesterday she had admitted that she never heard of Henry Wadsworth Longfellow — and Miss Brophy said he was one of the most famous American poets who had ever lived!

When I grow up, Addie thought, I won't be anything like Mother, all tired and worn out. I'll know all about poetry, and I'll have pretty clothes and my own land and my own schoolhouse, just like Miss Brophy.

Up until that moment, Mother had always seemed quite

perfect just the way she was. Addie felt guilty. She loved her mother, didn't she?

"Why are you looking at me like that, Addie?" Mother asked.

Addie felt her face go fiery red. What if Mother had somehow heard her thoughts? She cleared her throat nervously. "I was wondering," she said quickly, "do you think a woman could homestead a claim all by herself?"

"It's possible for a woman to homestead alone if she's got a tidy little sum of money laid by and good luck to go with it. I can't say it would be easy though," Mother replied, pinching the ends of the loaves and slipping them into greased pans. "She'd need to hire men to help with the breaking and the harvesting. There's just so many things that can go wrong. Now, why don't you recite your poem again?"

"Are you sure you want to hear it?"

"No!" Burt shouted, and put his hands over his ears. "We've heard that poem ten hundred times!"

"Go ahead, Addie. I love to hear you say it," Mother said encouragingly. She placed the rising loaves on the back of the stove and covered them with a cloth. "Don't be rude, Burton Grant."

Addie cleared her throat and tried not to look into her mother's eyes as she began to recite:

The Wild Prairie Rose

The wild prairie rose,
it blooms in the spring
along the slough,
where the long grass grows.
With blossoms sweet
and blossoms bright
it freights the wind with fragrance
all through the night.

"Very nice," Mother said, applauding. "I always enjoyed reciting when I was your age. Of course, I only got to go to real school for a year and a half."

"Why?" Addie asked.

"I've told you about when my mother died. I was twelve, just two years older than you, when the family was split up. There were ten of us altogether. The babies went to live with my oldest married sisters. The rest of us — three sisters and two brothers — traveled with my father from Wisconsin to Iowa to a new homestead." For a moment, Mother stared off into space.

"I never thought about how old you were when all that happened," Addie said. What a sad journey that must have been for Mother, with her own mother dead and half her brothers and sisters missing!

"It was a long, long time ago," Mother said, and smiled. "There's really not much to tell. When we left, that was the end of my schooling. I married your father three months after my sixteenth birthday. You were born a year later."

Maybe Mother knew a lot more about people than Addie realized. Maybe she could help her with the one thing that was bothering her most — what to do about Tilla.

"Mother, can I ask you something?" Addie said.

"Certainly." Mother pulled on her coat, mittens, and a pair of Pa's heavy boots. "Can you tell me while I get ready to go outside? I must see how many of our hens survived the storm."

Addie nodded, hoping George would stay in the root cellar a little longer. "Supposing there was this girl, and this girl was in trouble at school with some big boys who meant to throw rocks at her or break her arms off or worse."

Mother's eyes narrowed as she wrapped a thick, wool scarf around her neck. "Is this anyone I know?"

"No, no. It's just somebody from school."

"I see."

"And supposing," Addie continued quickly, "that to keep herself from being hurt she tells a lie that gets another girl in trouble instead."

"Is this other girl her friend?"

Addie shrugged. "Kind of a friend."

"The friend gets in serious trouble with these big boys? Do they hurt her?" Mother asked, buttoning her coat and tying a second scarf around her head and ears.

"Not exactly. You see, at the last minute the friend's brother comes and helps her. The big boys run away."

Mother was silent for a moment. "I think the girl who lied must tell her friend how sorry she is. To have a friend — even a *kind of* friend, as you say — means you have to *be* a friend, too. And it doesn't sound to me as if this girl who lied is behaving much like a friend."

Addie nodded. How simple and yet how difficult Mother's advice was! "But Mother, what will happen when the girl who lied says she's sorry?"

"It's worth the risk for her to find out. After all, a true friend knows how to forgive," Mother said. Just as she opened the door, Addie ran to her. She hugged Mother tightly, the way she hadn't in a long, long time.

"My goodness!" Mother exclaimed, and kissed Addie's forehead. "I'll be back soon. Now, will you watch over everyone?"

Addie watched Mother disappear out the door, shovel in hand, just as George came out of the root cellar. He banged the trap door shut and dumped corn on the table.

Lew and Burt had grown bored with bubbles and were beginning to wrestle on the floor. Nellie May looked ready to elbow her way right into the middle of the fight. "Stop!" Addie ordered, hauling Burt away from Lew. "Would you like me to read to you?"

"Yes! Read the circus one," Lew demanded. He pointed to the newspaper on the wall.

Addie knelt on the bed, searching *The Dakota Weekly Citizen*. With her head turned sideways, she read:

> An elephant belonging to Cooper, Jackson, and
> Company's circus escaped from its keeper at
> Elk Point, swam the Missouri River at that
> place, and is now roaming at large in Nebraska.

"How big is an elephant?" Lew demanded, the way he did every time she read the story.

"Very big. Bigger than an antelope. Bigger than a house. And mightily ferocious, with a long nose and ears that flap like huge blackbirds."

Her little brothers looked worried. "Where is Nebraska?" Burt asked in a little voice. "I hope it isn't close. Can we see it out the window?"

"It's a fair piece away," Addie said.

"Do you think we'll ever see one?" George asked quietly. The expression on his face was one Addie had never seen before. George looked so sad — as if he had lost something priceless, something he knew he'd never find again.

"Ever see an elephant?" Addie said, trying to make a joke. "He's probably clear across the country by now."

"No, you know I don't mean the elephant. I mean the antelope. Do you think we'll ever see antelope again?"

"George, if I said yes, I'd be lying," Addie said. Maybe if she changed the subject, she could cheer up George. She crouched near another spot on the wall and announced brightly, "What about this story over here? Let me read this. It's my very favorite."

"Oh, no. Not that 'madame' one again," Lew said, making a face. "I hate that dumb one."

Nellie May wriggled halfway under the trundle bed. Lew and Burt refused to listen. They charged about, holding their hands to their ears and waving their elbows like elephants' flapping ears.

Since George remained silent, Addie decided he might be interested. She read in a clear, expressive voice:

> Madame Lambert gave a vexed little toss of
> her head — a gesture intended to be awfully
> annihilating to Mr. Rupert Chessington,
> standing on the lower level of the piazza at
> Sea Spray House.

She loved the words *vexed* and *gesture* and *annihilating* and *piazza*. She especially loved *piazza*, although she had no idea what it, or the other words, meant. She just enjoyed the sound — exotic and far away and mysterious. *Piazza*. Piazza was exactly the kind of word she wished she had used in her poem except that it did not rhyme with *slough* or *bright*.

George still looked unhappy. He wasn't thinking about Mr. Rupert Chessington or his piazza. He was thinking about how this was probably one of the worst days of his life.

"George," Addie asked, "what's the matter?"

"Why can't you leave me alone? Why do you always have to ask me questions?" he demanded. "Everyone's always asking me questions. 'What did you do today at school, George?' or 'Who are your friends, George?' or 'Why are you always in trouble, George?' It's none of anyone's business!" He slammed an ear of corn on the table.

Her brother's face was filled with anger and sadness all at once, as if his whole world had come crashing down on him.

"Why don't you and one of the other nice boys your age memorize a poem together to say out loud for Miss Brophy's program?" Addie suggested. "I can help you practice."

George stared at his sister in disbelief. Couldn't she see how boring and babyish all those boys his age were? Compared to Daniel and Malcolm, they were as timid and dull-witted as sheep. Nobody except a Connolly would think of putting a firecracker down the outhouse two-holer. Nobody except a Connolly would think of walking halfway to school upside down, with his shoes on his hands. Memorizing a poem was something a Connolly would never do. "I don't want to learn any silly poem," George said.

"You could learn a song."

"I don't want to sing any silly song."

"Well, what *do* you want to do?"

"I wish...I wish," he replied, his voice growing softer so Addie could barely hear, "I wish that I could make those pronghorn come alive again."

George turned quickly away to look out the window. If the antelope could come back to life, he would run away with them and be free. He'd stay outdoors forever where he could breathe and run and shout. He'd never again go into a dull, airless classroom where he would be made to feel like a fool and a failure because he was still in the first reader and had to sit with the littlest children.

Addie could not think of any words to comfort him. She reached out to touch his shoulder. He was trembling. And although she could not see his face, she knew that her brother was crying.

9   A REAL CHRISTMAS TREE

Wind blew through the schoolhouse floorboards and rattled the tin smokestack. On the tenth morning after the blizzard, Addie, George, and the other students sat on benches and swung their stout shoes and boots back and forth, back and forth. It was hard to sit still. On the long walks to school, even boots that had been carefully greased with hog lard did not protect the children's feet from the dampness or the cold. Their toes were often covered with chilblains that first numbed, then burned. Ill-fitting flannel underwear and heavy stockings scratched.

The schoolroom smelled unpleasantly of dirty, wet wool. It was too hot near the stove and too cold along the walls. The wooden benches were uncomfortable, and even though Addie liked school, sometimes it seemed as if the day went very slowly.

There were six empty seats again today. They belonged

to Conrad Shaver, Tommy Owens, Herbert Bradbury, Malcolm Connolly, Daniel Connolly, and Tilla Bergstrom. Herbert and Tommy were both home with a mild case of croup. Conrad was in bed with a bad earache. Everyone knew why the Connolly boys had not returned. Their pa did not care that they'd been expelled. He told Miss Brophy he had wasted enough of everyone's time trying to thrash an education into his sons' thick hides. As soon as the weather broke, he planned to hire out Malcolm and Daniel for farm work.

Tilla's absence remained a mystery. Every day Miss Brophy called Tilla's name, and every day Addie twisted around in her seat, hoping to see that pale blue kerchief and those proud, laughing eyes. But she never did.

"Does anyone know what has happened to Tilla? I think her brother would bring me a message if something were wrong. She was doing so well. I don't understand why she has stopped coming," Miss Brophy said, marking the tenth black x next to Tilla's name in the roll book.

No one raised a hand. None of the children had ever visited the Norwegian settlement on Ree Heights. It was said to be a desolate stretch past a row of battered cottonwoods along Dry Creek. There, two or three Norwegian families had taken up one-hundred-sixty-acre homesteads. They kept to themselves.

"Addie, have you seen or heard from Tilla?" Miss Brophy

asked. "Do you know where she lives on Ree Heights?"

"Yes, ma'am, I think so," Addie said quickly. "She showed me once when she visited my house. I saved the map we made, just in case I ever visited her." Addie wanted to be helpful. At the same time, she felt awkward and guilty. She longed to stand up and confess, "I think I know why Tilla's not here." She had betrayed her friend and put her in terrible danger. Tilla didn't even realize she was safe now that Daniel and Malcolm weren't ever coming back.

Addie knew what she must do. She raised her hand.

"Yes, Addie?" Miss Brophy said.

Addie cleared her throat. "Maybe I could go to Ree Heights to take Tilla the work she's missed."

"That's very thoughtful of you, Addie. And you could remind her about our Christmas program, especially since it's only one day away," Miss Brophy said. "Are you sure you know the way?"

Addie nodded as convincingly as she could.

"Well, I think that's a fine idea. If Tilla does not return tomorrow, you may go during class."

It *was* a fine idea, Addie thought. She felt a little better already.

Miss Brophy closed the roll book and took off her glasses. "Speaking of our Christmas program, how many of you have ever seen a real Christmas tree?"

The children squirmed and whispered. Christmas trees! This sounded better than sums or geography.

"Come now," Miss Brophy smiled encouragingly at a few puzzled faces. "Someone must have seen a Christmas tree once."

Most of the children hadn't seen an evergreen tree since settling in Dakota. Christmas to many homesteading families was just another day. There simply wasn't money to spare for gifts, fancy dinners, or decorations.

On her first Christmas morning in Dakota, Addie had missed the beautiful, ornamented pine they always had back in Sabula. At Oak Hollow her family celebrated just with fragrant red apples Pa brought from Scotland. Addie had shined her beautiful apple and saved it until it nearly went soft.

"I remember one Christmas tree we had a long, long time ago," Fred Falkenberg said. "But that was back in Michigan before we came here. It was green and tall and pointy, and it was on fire."

The class laughed.

"This year you will all have the opportunity to see a real Christmas tree," Miss Brophy said. "We are going to make our own decorations and have a tree in our classroom for our program."

Everyone started talking at once.

"But where will you find one, Miss Brophy?" Donald Feeney asked. "Christmas trees don't grow in Dakota."

Addie was puzzled, too. Except for a few cottonwoods and bur oaks, there weren't any genuine trees in Dakota.

"How will a tree fit?" Lorenzo Hebbert asked. "Won't it go through the roof?"

"I'll take care of the tree," she said. "What you are going to do this morning is work on the decorations."

Everyone cheered. They forgot about chilblains and itchy stockings. Addie looked at Tilla's empty seat again. Tilla was missing everything.

The children worked in groups stringing popcorn and cutting and sewing small bags from sheets of white mosquito netting. These, they were thrilled to learn, would hold real hard candy that Miss Brophy had purchased for each of them with her own money.

"Isn't Miss Brophy wonderful?" Addie whispered to her brother, who was staring at the ceiling.

"Nope. Christmas decorations are stupid," George grumbled.

"Christmas decorations are *not* stupid. *You* are stupid," Addie hissed as she tied a string to a candy bag. She was outraged that her sullen brother could not appreciate Miss Brophy's generosity. Since the Connolly brothers had gone away, George acted worse than ever. He moped and complained. He was even unwilling to play games with the other boys.

"Do you need some help, George?" Miss Brophy asked kindly. George did not answer. He just kept staring at the ceiling. The other children laughed and talked as they folded rustling red and green tissue paper into stars and bent pieces of wire to be used as candle holders. "Can I show you how to cut out a ship with scissors? I bet you would be very good at that."

George folded his arms defiantly across his chest.

"You don't have to make a ship. You can make anything you'd like."

"What about an animal?" Addie suggested. "George knows a lot about animals. He watches them all the time. Maybe he could make a bird or a Christmas donkey, just like in the Bible story."

George scowled at his sister. "Well, all right," he said unenthusiastically, picking up a pair of scissors.

Disappointment flitted across Miss Brophy's face. Now look what George has gone and done, Addie thought angrily. He's hurt Miss Brophy's feelings.

"That's all right if you don't want to help with the decorations," Miss Brophy replied. "I have another job that needs to be done — one that requires a strong fellow. Put on your coat and follow me. While I'm gone, Addie, you are in charge of the classroom. You may sit at my desk and make sure no one misbehaves."

George looked surprised that his teacher wanted his help. He pulled on his hat with the mule-ear flaps, buttoned his coat, and followed Miss Brophy outdoors. Addie proudly took Miss Brophy's seat behind her desk.

"What are they doing out there?" Myra Renshaw asked, tiptoeing to the frost-covered window. "I can't see."

"Please take your seat," Addie said, rapping the desk with the ruler, just like a real teacher. She enjoyed seeing the room from this position. She felt very important. To please Miss Brophy, she thoroughly wiped the new blackboard. She arranged Miss Brophy's pencils in an empty tomato can.

When Miss Brophy and George reappeared, their cheeks were flushed pink from the cold, and their coats were covered with snow. They dragged in a large wooden washtub filled with loose dirt. For once, George was smiling.

"What's that?" Lucia Hebbert asked.

"You'll see," Miss Brophy said with a wink. She and George pushed the heavy tub into a corner of the room.

"I chopped the Christmas tree," he whispered smugly as he sat down beside Addie. "All by myself."

Addie did not know whether to believe him or not. There had been no evergreen trees near the school last time she looked. What was George talking about?

After lunch, Miss Brophy led the class in Christmas carols. Ordinarily, George refused to sing because Malcolm once told him all school songs were babyish. But this time he joined in on "Oh come let us adore Him," much louder than Addie thought necessary. Since he seemed so pleased with himself, she didn't say anything.

When the singing practice ended, Gunther and Emma Schuler draped green paper chains around the doorway. Rolfe and Emile used fishline to hang stars made from silver-foil cigar wrappers. Maude and Lucy Hoopes drew a forest scene on the blackboard, complete with mountains and a waterfall they remembered from their home in eastern Kentucky. In perfect script above the lovely landscape, Donald Feeney wrote, "Merry Christmas to all our families."

Addie wondered if the mountains on the blackboard were like the ones Tilla had left behind in Norway. If Tilla's mother came to the program and saw the beautiful picture, maybe she wouldn't feel so homesick.

Much too quickly, it was time to go home.

"Addie and George!" one of the children shouted. "Your pa's here!" Pa was waiting outside. The sleigh was heaped with blankets and a heavy buffalo robe.

"George can ride with Pa, Miss Brophy. Please can't I stay and help you put up the rest of the decorations? There's still so much to do," Addie pleaded.

"I could certainly use your help. Perhaps if it's all right with your father, I could give you a ride home in my sleigh," Miss Brophy said. She tramped outside to ask.

Pa gave his permission, and George and the last group of noisy children disappeared. Miss Brophy went outside again. Suddenly, Addie heard her teacher's voice calling, "Addie, Addie! Open the door, please."

Addie ran to the door, and there was Miss Brophy dragging two cedar scrubs in each hand. Addie helped her carry in four more of the little bushes. They were stubby and had short green needles. "Is this the Christmas tree George chopped?" she asked.

"Yes," Miss Brophy replied, pulling off her mittens. "And I hope my idea works, or twenty-one children will be very disappointed. Can you hand me that rope over there?"

Addie nodded. She had no idea how her teacher could make a Christmas tree with scrubs and rope, but she did as she was told. Together they fastened one end of a long rope to a nail in the ceiling. The other end was anchored around the tub of sand. With smaller pieces of rope, they tied each cedar scrub to the next in a kind of relay, one atop the other, from the ceiling to the tub.

Miss Brophy stood back to admire their work. "It's beginning to look like a real Dakota Christmas tree, don't you think?"

"It's the most beautiful Christmas tree I've ever seen," Addie said.

Addie began draping garlands of popcorn from branch to branch. Miss Brophy stood on tiptoe on a chair to place a star made from an old Christmas card at the top. All the while they decorated the scrubs with dangling candy bags, stars, ships, and candy sticks, Miss Brophy talked and laughed. "If my parents and four brothers could only see me now!" Miss Brophy said. "When I left New York, they were certain I wouldn't last. They said Dakota was too far away, too wild, and too unfriendly. They said I'd get homesick and come back on the train by Christmas."

"Do you ever feel homesick?" Addie asked.

"Not very often. I suppose I was most lonely the first time I left home and went to boarding school to get my teacher's certificate."

"Sometimes I like to make believe I'm a teacher," Addie confided.

"You do? Well, maybe you'll be a teacher, too, when you grow up."

Miss Brophy's open smile encouraged Addie. She found herself telling Miss Brophy that she was afraid of lightning storms and that she thought chocolates that came from Schlissman's store in Scotland were better than those from anywhere else. She even told Miss Brophy about Ruby Lillian.

As they talked, it seemed to Addie that Miss Brophy wasn't her teacher anymore. Instead, Miss Brophy seemed almost like the best friend Addie had longed for — someone to tell all kinds of secrets to, someone wise who would always listen and never laugh or make fun of her.

"Did you ever have a very best friend when you were my age?" Addie asked as she bent the wire holders around candle stubs.

Miss Brophy stopped hooking paper hearts to branches. "Oh, yes. Her name was Lucille McDermott. She and I used to do everything, go everywhere together. She could ride bareback faster and laugh louder than anyone I ever knew. She had a lot of wild energy that used to get her into trouble. Once she tipped over the outhouse with somebody locked inside, and another time she ice-skated through the frozen streets wearing a shocking bloomer outfit!" Miss Brophy laughed. "And when she was quiet and thinking — as she often had to be in school — she used to chew on the end of her long braid. That made my teacher, Miss Schocken, very angry. 'Bad habits! Bad habits!' she'd shout."

"And what did Lucille do then?" Addie asked.

"She would chew her hair secretly, when the teacher wasn't looking." Miss Brophy laughed. "Just to make her mad, I used to call her 'Toothy Lucy,' because she was always biting the end of her braid."

"And even though she chewed her hair and did those other wild things, she was your very best friend?"

Miss Brophy smiled when she saw the confused look on Addie's face. "She was. Lucy had many fine qualities. She was generous and very good at inventing all kinds of games. You know, there really is no such thing as a perfect friend."

"I suppose you're right," Addie said slowly. She thought about how Eleanor used to shock her with reckless practical jokes back in Iowa. And yet, she and Eleanor had remained friends through it all.

Miss Brophy stepped back to admire the tree. "You can hardly tell it's cedar scrubs unless you look closely, don't you think? I hope the children will like it."

"I know they will," Addie said. The tree was something else to tell Tilla about. She would try to persuade Tilla to come to the Christmas program to see the most beautiful tree in all of Hutchinson County.

When it was time to go home, Addie helped Miss Brophy prepare the stove for the morning. Together, they filled two more buckets with coal. The embers were cold, and the schoolroom was growing chilly. Miss Brophy checked her pocket watch. "I hope your parents won't be worrying," she said. "We'd better hurry."

The sky was mottled orange, the color of the sun hanging

low on the horizon. Even the snow seemed to reflect the glow. Miss Brophy's horse, Nell, was waiting patiently in the shed beside the schoolhouse. Addie admired how quickly her teacher harnessed the horse. "I convinced the school board to build a shed so I could keep Nell and my sleigh here. It's a long way to the Madsons', where I board. It's easier to have my own horse than beg for rides when the weather's too cold for walking." She flipped the reins. "Come on, Nell, we're going to show Addie a surprise."

Addie sat wrapped in a heavy blanket, watching the prairie fly past. The cold air stung her nose. She was glad she wasn't walking. After a few minutes, they came to a low rise. Miss Brophy pulled the reins. "Here it is," she said proudly.

Addie squinted, but all she could see was more snow and a tiny tar paper shack in the distance. Where was the surprise?

"It's my land," Miss Brophy said. "How do you like it?"

"Very nice," Addie said politely, imagining a frame house with a lovely front parlor.

"I hired someone to help me break twenty acres, and in the spring, after the snow melts, I intend to break twenty more and sow sod corn. And I'm going to plant a vegetable garden, too. I'll grow pumpkins, peas, beans, tomatoes — just like the gardens we used to have at home," she said, her eyes shining. "It will be wonderful, don't you think? And

111

in a few years I'll build up a small herd of cattle. You can't see it now, but this is some of the best grassland around."

Miss Brophy shook Nell's reins, and the sleigh bumped along toward Oak Hollow. Addie stole a glance at her teacher. Miss Brophy's enthusiasm for Dakota reminded Addie of Pa's. "It's the Land of Begin Again," Addie said, echoing the words she had heard her father use so often. "Anything's possible."

"That's it!" Miss Brophy exclaimed. "My family seems to think a woman on her own can't do what I'm doing. Maybe one day, when I've got my real house built, then they'll see. I mean to stay. Addie, you are special. You understand."

Even though no one else was there to hear Miss Brophy's compliment, Addie smiled. Miss Brophy thought she was special. All the way home, Addie scarcely felt the cold.

10   REE HEIGHTS

Addie waved to the faces pressed against the steaming schoolhouse windows. The children and the Christmas decorations were so crowded together that it was difficult to see anyone clearly. She thought she caught a glimpse of George, frowning as though he wished Mother and Pa had given permission for him to escape, too.

"Be careful, Addie! Hurry straight home from Tilla's house!" Miss Brophy called from the doorway, peering at the sky. The morning seemed almost balmy compared to the cold weather of the day before. Every now and again, the sun appeared and disappeared behind the clouds.

Addie's cheeks were flushed. She unbuttoned her coat and wished she'd left her heavy scarf and mittens behind. She had studied Tilla's map carefully, and now she was on her way to Ree Heights with the song sheet and Miss Brophy's note for Tilla and her parents. Happily, she made three giant leaps along the hard-packed wagon road. Then she reached inside her apron pocket and pulled out Ruby Lillian.

"While all the other children are trapped inside school for the rest of the day, we get to go on a very important errand," she told her smiling doll. She put Ruby Lillian back into her pocket where she'd be comfortable. Addie felt grown-up and responsible and free to do whatever she pleased.

Ree Heights was a good hour's walk. Addie had plenty of time to practice her apology to Tilla. But when she thought about what she would say, her light-heartedness quickly disappeared. "Hello, Tilla! How are you?" She nodded to a limp pile of dead grass sticking out of the snow.

No. That wouldn't do.

Addie cleared her throat. "Tilla, we all missed you so much. Why haven't you come back? You'll never guess. The Connolly boys have left school for good. Isn't that wonderful?"

She frowned. Those weren't the words she really wanted to say. Tilla probably hated her. Maybe she shouldn't be on this errand after all. Tilla probably didn't ever want to see her or hear how sorry she was about her lie to the Connolly boys.

Addie stopped and stared absently at the heel marks she had made in the snow. They looked like little frowns. What if she just hid the homework and the invitation to the program? No one would know she had never made the trip to Ree Heights.

She hesitated before taking another step. Of course, all Miss Brophy would have to do would be to take one look at her face. She'd know immediately that Addie had lied. There was no way out. She had to go to Ree Heights and ask for Tilla's forgiveness, no matter how hard it was.

Addie trudged past the slough. Not far away, she could see a group of knobby hills. Wind had blown the hilltops clear of snow, leaving behind melting, muddy patches that reminded her of skin showing through the hair on a balding man's head.

How far was it to the place where she should cross the Jim River? She remembered Tilla had drawn cottonwood trees on the map. Was that the grove ahead? She slid down a drift toward the frozen river. The warmer weather had thawed only the edges. Carefully, she made her way across the ice.

Beyond the cottonwoods on the other side was a field where the snow lay undisturbed. Every step made a loud crunch as her boot broke through the brittle top layer. The noise of shattering snow was pleasant, almost musical. Addie moved her feet in and out to different rhythms. "Ah-one-ah-two-ah-one-two-three! Ah-one-two-three, on my knee!" she sang loudly, so absorbed in her snow-stepping game that she didn't notice the sun had disappeared. The air was colder. Loose, sharp particles of snow blew suddenly skyward in a twirling wind devil. Addie glanced up and shivered.

In the distance smoke curled. Could it be from Tilla's home? Atop the next low rise, Addie looked all around. She could find no trace of the big, white house Tilla had once bragged was even taller and more impressive than the new schoolhouse. Addie could see only two hastily built, windowless dugouts — not much more than caves shoveled from a steep embankment. Each had a curious door constructed with wood scraps, burlap, and flattened cracker tins. Nowhere in sight was a barn or any sign of the thousand cows and two thousand pigs Tilla claimed her uncle next door owned. Addie did not even spy one chicken. She sniffed the air. There was no aroma of delicious baking cakes or roasting meats — food a king's former chef would surely cook.

If Tilla lived here, she was poor, not rich. Were most of her stories plain fantasy, just as Addie had suspected all along? Why did Tilla tell such lies? Was it because her real life was so hard?

Near the dugouts were several open cutters, a sleigh, and one makeshift sled built from an old wagon box. Did Tilla's family have company? From inside one dugout, Addie could hear singing. The songs reminded her of church hymns, except that the words weren't English. And it wasn't Sunday.

"Maybe Norwegians celebrate a different Sabbath," Addie whispered, nervously patting her doll. When the strange music stopped, she knocked softly on the door.

No one answered.

She knocked again. The door swung open slowly, and a woman peered out. Her sad, sagging expression startled Addie.

"Hello," Addie said in her most friendly voice. "Can you tell me where Tilla Bergstrom's family lives?"

The woman did not reply. The careworn creases around her mouth gave the impression that she had not smiled in years.

"My name is Addie Mills. Do you speak English? Does anyone here speak English?"

The woman glanced nervously over her shoulder.

"TILLA BERGSTROM," Addie repeated, louder. "Do you know her?"

A man's low voice came from behind the door. He wasn't using words Addie understood, but she could tell from his tone that he was asking the sad woman a question. She disappeared. The man stepped outside. He was dressed in black like the traveling preacher Addie had seen last spring. His high, ruddy cheekbones and bushy dark eyebrows framed sorrowful eyes. He, too, looked as if he had not smiled in a long time.

"Please, sir, can you tell me if Tilla Bergstrom lives here?" Addie asked again.

He nodded silently, took Addie firmly by the elbow, and guided her inside. She glanced about, her eyes slowly growing accustomed to the dim candlelight.

The smoky, dark room was hot and cramped. Several people were weeping loudly, and a baby wailed. Addie wondered how so many adults and children could fit into such a small house. Grown-ups stood quietly or sat in chairs, the men on one side of the room, the women on the other. There was something happening here that was frightening yet familiar. She knew she did not want to be in this place.

"Please, I think there's a mistake. I don't want to come in," Addie insisted. But the man in black would not let go of her elbow. He kept walking slowly toward the other end of the room. She did not wish to be rude and kept moving reluctantly along. "I can come back another time," Addie tried again. "I didn't mean to interrupt."

The man stopped. A group of women with red eyes parted and let Addie through. Immediately, she saw the thing she feared most.

Resting over two sawhorses was a long wooden coffin.

Addie trembled. She wanted to turn and run, but there was no escape. Tilla. It must be Tilla who was in there. Why else had the man in black brought her here when Addie had said Tilla's name?

The room began to spin. Addie had to look. She had to be sure. But somehow she couldn't. It was too terrible.

The man in black announced something in Norwegian, and everyone bowed their heads. Addie could tell they were

118

praying. She folded her hands, but when she closed her eyes, she felt even dizzier. She opened her eyes slightly and recognized a white blond head. Ole was hunched over and sobbing into his big, wide hands. He was sobbing for his sister.

Standing beside Ole were two teenaged girls. The eyes of the girl holding pretty Katya were red and swollen. The toddler chewed on her dress sash and looked about in confusion. The other girl had a hard, dry-eyed expression, as if she couldn't cry anymore.

Addie's eyes filled with tears. I'm too late, she thought. Too late to tell Tilla I'm sorry.

Suddenly, a sooty-faced toddler bolted past, knocking Addie off-balance. She stumbled forward, close enough to peer into the coffin.

There, looking as if she were only asleep, was a woman. Her face was pale. Her cheeks looked sunken. Cradled peacefully in one arm was a tiny baby.

Addie stepped back as fast as she could. Every time she and her family had attended funerals in Sabula, the same nightmarish dread overwhelmed her. What if the dead person sat up? What if the corpse grabbed her? In desperation, she tried to remember the direction of the door. Someone touched her shoulder. She jumped. Quickly, she turned.

It was Tilla. Tilla, alive and breathing!

Addie threw her arms around her friend's neck and cried and cried as if her heart would break.

"Come outside here for some air," Tilla whispered hoarsely. People stepped aside to let the girls pass. Tilla led Addie outside and into the other dugout.

Addie sunk exhausted onto a bench. The air was cooler, fresher in this soddy. No one else was here except an old woman, who was carefully arranging a table with strange, flat bread, a few chunks of cheese, and a small tin of oily-smelling fish — hardly enough food for everyone. The woman said nothing but handed Addie a mug of strong black coffee.

"Drink some," Tilla said.

Addie's hands shook as she lifted the mug to her lips, but her dizziness disappeared. She looked at Tilla to make sure her friend wasn't a dream.

It was true. Tilla was sitting beside her. Her kerchief was dark blue, and she wore a fancy, clean apron Addie had never seen before. A black shawl was tied around her thin, bent shoulders. Tilla's face was gaunt. There were circles under her eyes, which no longer flashed blue and defiant. Now they were as dull and somber as the winter sky.

"Who...was that in there?" Addie whispered.

Tilla bit her lip and bowed her head. "Mama and da new baby."

Addie took a deep breath and let the air out slowly. She did not know what to say except, "I'm sorry."

"She vas sick and had to stay in bed. I miss school to help. Da baby lived enough to be named. Iver Knute. Dat's all. I hardly knew him," Tilla said slowly. "Now Mama's gone. I have to stay home for da oder little ones. No more school, Papa says. He needs me here." She lifted her chin in the same proud, stubborn gesture that used to make Addie so angry. Addie knew Tilla did not want her pity.

How would Tilla get along without her mother — the lonely, homesick woman who wept and wept and refused to learn English because she knew she'd always be a stranger in Dakota? Who would tell the old Norwegian tales Tilla liked so much? What would it be like for Tilla and Katya and Ole and their other brothers and sisters without their mother's singing?

Tilla's older sisters had their jobs in town. Tilla would have to cook and clean and sew and take care of the youngest children — more than could be expected of one willow-thin girl only nine years old. There was no choice. Her family needed her.

Addie sighed. If Tilla never came back to school, who would play make-believe? Who would share special picnics? Nobody. Except for Ruby Lillian, Addie would be alone and friendless again, the same way she was before Tilla walked through the schoolroom door. It wasn't fair. Nothing seemed fair. Nothing had worked out the way Addie had planned.

Tilla blew her nose. Addie still could not think of anything comforting to say. Her mind was filled with memories of the day Nellie May was born. What if Mother had died? What if Nellie had died, too? And suddenly Addie wanted more than anything to leap up and run home with Ruby Lillian, far away from Tilla and this sad place. She had to see if her family was all right. She had to know for certain no harm had come to them.

"I have to go now," Addie said. "It's getting late, and my parents will worry." She handed Tilla the crumpled homework and the Christmas program invitation. "I brought these for you. The program is tonight. But I suppose you won't be able..."

"No, tink not."

"Well, goodbye, Tilla," Addie said sadly. She turned to leave.

"Vait!" Tilla called. She ran to the table, then hurried back to Addie with something in her hands. "Take some *flotbrod* vit you. It's a long vay. You be hungry."

"Thank you, Tilla," Addie said, even though she did not really want to take the foreign-looking food. But she tucked the bread inside her apron pocket, next to Ruby Lillian. She buttoned her coat, glad after all that she had not left her mittens and scarf at school. A light snow was beginning to fall.

"Goodbye, Addie!" Tilla called.

"Goodbye, Tilla!" Addie waved. She walked quickly to keep warm. Suddenly, she stopped. She had forgotten to tell Tilla she was sorry. What if she never had another chance to apologize for the lie she had told to the Connolly brothers? Addie turned. But at that moment, the man in black emerged from the other dugout. He pointed to the sky and motioned for Addie to return. He was shouting something.

He wants me to go back to the funeral, Addie thought. I'll never go in that dugout again. I'm going home.

She ran as fast as she could away from Ree Heights. The most direct route back to Oak Hollow was the way Tilla had come when she visited. Addie decided to go the same way, across the Jim River, past the railroad tracks, and the telegraph poles. Cold lashed at her face and hands. As she started through the field near the grove of cottonwoods, she retraced some of her old path. Already her footprints were nearly filled with new snow. She rested a minute to think. Would she be able to recognize the snow-covered landmarks? The wind had shifted from the northwest. Across the western horizon, a black smudge of clouds grew like spilled ink. More snow on the way, sure enough.

"We'll be home in no time," she assured Ruby Lillian.

But with every step, the snow became more blinding. She could see only a few feet ahead. Now she was heading into the wind, which had suddenly picked up speed. What if she wasn't going southwest anymore? She longed to be home; she wouldn't turn back. Addie stopped to wrap her scarf over her mouth and nose to make it easier to breathe. She rubbed her eyes with her mitten to brush away ice that clung to her lashes and froze her eyelids shut.

For what seemed to be miles, she fought against the wind and snow, uncertain where she and Ruby Lillian were. The railroad tracks she had expected to cross were gone. Not one telegraph pole appeared. Out of the howling white she heard low, anguished bellows. There must be cows nearby. Hadn't Pa once told her that a blizzard can make herds go blind? Maybe these animals were lost, too. Cows caught in a blizzard kept moving along together. Eventually, they trapped themselves in hollows or fence corners, where they suffocated or froze to death in rising drifts. The very idea made Addie feel desperate.

How would she ever find her way home? She reached out her arms. If there were cows, maybe there was a fence. If there was a fence, perhaps she could follow it to a farm. She could find shelter there until Pa came to get her. She groped in the wind and snow. Nothing. Her eyes were freezing shut again. She rubbed them with her mittens and kept walking.

11 SNOWBOUND!

As the storm approached, a dead calm settled over the children playing in the schoolyard. The younger ones, who had been shrieking and chasing each other around the brand new flagpole, now stood silent, transfixed. The boys George's age, who had red faces and hair matted flat with sweat, abandoned their game of follow-the-leader over the drifts. Fred Falkenberg, Donald Feeney, and the two Shaver brothers stared at the eerie western horizon.

"It's like a wall. A white wall," said six-year-old Myra Renshaw.

"That ain't no wall," George said in a superior voice. "Walls don't move."

The enormous cloud rolled closer and closer until it was upon them, bursting with wet, fat flakes so thick that no one could see. The wind howled, and the temperature plummeted. The shivering children dove for hats, coats, and mittens discarded earlier.

"Come inside, everyone!" Miss Brophy called. She rang the bell as hard as she could, counting the children as they scrambled through the door. There were supposed to be seventeen students today — sixteen, with Addie gone. She counted only fifteen. "Someone's missing. Where's George?"

"He's still outside."

When Miss Brophy stepped outdoors, the wind whipped her skirt around her legs. She cupped her hands to her mouth and over the roar of the storm shouted, "George! Where are you? Come in!"

"What about Addie?" George shouted back, huddled against the schoolhouse. "I have to go get Addie."

"You come inside. She's all right. She's probably already safe at home by now. Come inside!"

Reluctantly, George stomped the snow from his boots and brushed his coat in the doorway. His teacher was trying to sound confident, but she knew this was no ordinary snowstorm. George could see that plain enough on her frightened face. He could hardly bear to look at Miss Brophy. He knew they were both thinking of what might be happening to his sister out there.

Miss Brophy struggled to bolt the door so that it would not blow open. She turned to George and said quietly, "You're the oldest boy in class today, and I'm going to need your help. As you can see, we must be as brave as we can."

George tried to feel brave, but he couldn't. He looked about the room and saw that the children who weren't crying were nervously standing on tiptoe, pushing and shoving, trying to peer out the windows to see if their parents were coming to take them home. There was nothing to see. With a terrific blast of wind behind it, snow had blanketed all the windows. Panes of glass shook and rattled as if someone on the outside were trying to get in. Little Lena buried her head in her sister's skirt to muffle the noise.

Maybe just for now, George thought, I can pretend I'm brave.

"There there, Lena," Miss Brophy said, gently smoothing her tangled curls. "Why don't we all gather around and sing Christmas carols? As soon as the storm lets up, I'm sure your mothers and fathers will come for you. Until then, let's try and be as cozy as possible."

While the children sang, George tied one end of a long rope to the doorknob and the other end around his waist. He went outside to the little shed and pitched as much hay as he could for Miss Brophy's horse. Poor Nell! He covered her back with a saddle blanket and hoped she wouldn't freeze to death. Her tail was already coated thick with ice. She shook her head and rubbed her muzzle against her front leg to knock away the ice around her nostrils and eyes. Snow sifted into the shed from every direction.

Three times George filled the bucket with coal and staggered into the wind. He used the rope to pull himself back to the schoolhouse door, where Miss Brophy met him and took the coal inside. George calculated a dozen more buckets of coal might remain in the shed. On his fourth trip, something brushed against his leg. It was a pheasant, desperate to escape the storm. George watched helplessly as the bird stumbled into the shed, collapsed, and died.

"George, are you all right?" Miss Brophy called.

The children gasped when they saw George, covered with snow, his face bright red. "Now I'll show you a good trick," he said cheerfully, all the time trying to shake the vision of the dead bird. He took off his frozen coat and placed it in the corner of the room. "See what my magic coat can do. It stands all by itself!"

The children applauded and laughed. Even Lena smiled.

George knew a Dakota blizzard might maroon them for days. When he replaced the coal bucket near the shelf in the corner of the room, he was relieved to see the three boxes of crackers, a dozen tins of oysters, four fresh loaves of bread, and fragrant cobbler made from dried apples — all the food for the oyster supper that was supposed to have been held that night. On what Miss Brophy called her "trouble shelf," George counted two blankets, three tins of peaches, and three of corn, a box of hardtack, a bag of rice, some cocoa, a few tins of condensed milk, a small bag of flour, two saucepans, and a handful of spoons, forks, and knives. These were supplies no student was ever allowed to touch. Hanging on the wall beside the shelf was a pair of snowshoes. "We must be ready for the day we have an emergency," Miss Brophy had warned.

That day had arrived.

12   HAVEN IN THE STORM

A blast of wind hurtled Addie backward across a patch of ice, plunging her into what seemed a bottomless drift. Struggling to stand, she fell again into the waist-high snow. She groped about on her hands and knees, terrified she might have lost Ruby Lillian. One of her mittens fell off. Her eyes were almost frozen shut, but she staggered to her feet. Before she could check her pocket, the wind slammed her against something solid.

Addie embraced the wall as if it were an old, lost friend. Was it part of a house? Where was the door? She ran her hand along the flat surface. There was no light visible and no sound to be heard except the shrieking wind. When she followed the wall to a corner, she came face to face with an enormous drift and was forced to retrace her steps.

This time she set off in the other direction. At last she found a crack. Following the crack up and down with her hands, she realized it *was* a door. She wedged the toe of her boot inside the opening and grasped the door with both hands. With all her might, she gave a yank. When nothing happened, she dug away more snow from the base of the door. Again she tugged and at last pulled open a gap just wide enough for her to slip inside. She pulled the door to close it again.

In the darkness Addie smelled wet hay, damp wood, and steaming dung. She was inside someone's barn. She leaned with a great sigh of relief against the wall, then fumbled inside her apron pocket. Had she lost Ruby Lillian? Her hands were nearly numb, but she thought she could feel something hard and round. There was her doll, surrounded by a cushion of crumbled bread! She tucked Ruby Lillian back in her pocket.

A bell rattled, and hooves stamped against the cold ground. Addie could hear the familiar labored sound of a cow breathing. Something hurried past her leg, squawking. Chickens were in here, too. "At least we won't be all alone, Ruby Lillian," she said.

The owner had to come out eventually to feed these animals and do the milking. And then Addie would be discovered, and she could take her doll and go home to Oak Hollow.

The barn was cold. Addie was out of the wind but not out of danger. For a few minutes she rested. Her feet were beginning to feel dangerously numb — the first sign of frostbite. Although she was exhausted, she knew she had to keep moving. Wrapping her mittenless hand in her scarf for warmth, Addie marched in place, knees high, boots pounding against the barn floor. It was important to keep as awake and as warm as possible. During the last blizzard, she remembered Pa had warned, "The cold will kill you if you doze off."

There was little point trying to find the farmhouse. She could easily start walking in the wrong direction and become hopelessly lost. She and Ruby Lillian would be safe here.

Now that her eyes had adjusted to the darkness, she recognized the black shapes around her. She reached out and counted one, two, three cows. Even though she could not see them clearly, she wasn't frightened. Ever since she was six years old, she had done the milking, often in the semidarkness of early winter dawn. It was pleasantly familiar here. She almost felt as if she were home again.

Unlike Addie, who had been exposed to the terrible cold, the cows had been protected in the barn since the blizzard began. The strong, shaggy creatures were in no danger of freezing to death. But they made hungry lowing noises. Addie wondered when the last time was that they had been milked or given water.

"Hello. Our names are Addie and Ruby Lillian," she

announced, the way polite guests are supposed to. "What are yours?" She went over to one cow and pressed her cheek against its dusty, warm back. The cow didn't seem to mind. "I will call you Old No Horn, just like Anna and Mr. Fency's cow. That way we'll already seem like old friends."

Addie walked carefully about, trying to determine just how this barn was arranged. How she longed for a lantern or a box of matches! She stumbled upon something hard — a ladder. There might be a hayloft overhead. Hay would make a warm place to stay.

Cautiously, Addie pulled herself up each rung. Although it seemed warmer up here near the top of the barn, the hay was damp and soggy. Melting ice from the ceiling dripped and trickled down her collar. Snow blew through cracks in the roof. No, she and Ruby Lillian would not stay in the loft.

Addie's coat was beginning to thaw. It felt heavy and uncomfortably wet, yet she didn't dare to take it off. She could still feel her fingers and toes. That was important. They weren't frozen. Yet.

She made several trips up and down the ladder carrying bundles of hay under her arm. "Here, Old No Horn," she called. "Dinner for you and your friends." She could feel the cows' warm breath on her hands and hear their eager munching.

Addie went to work arranging her own pile of hay in the corner of the barn farthest from the draft near the door. Two ducks greeted her angrily and flapped away. "Sorry to take your spot," Addie said. She covered herself with hay although she knew she could not allow herself to close her eyes. If she fell asleep here, no one might find her until it was too late. She'd freeze to death in her sleep.

She was so anxious about dozing off that she did not dare rest for long. Her arms and knees ached and her teeth were chattering, but she climbed out of the hay. She stamped her feet and beat her hands together, counting up to two hundred. She wished she had something to do, something to think about besides the cold and dark.

She reached in her pocket to pull out Ruby Lillian, and there was some of the bread Tilla had given her. Most of it had fallen out, and what was left was crushed. Addie nibbled all along one edge, careful to save the rest for later. "This Norwegian bread doesn't taste like much, but it's better than nothing," she told her doll. Her stomach growled loudly. How long would the storm last? When would the farmer come to feed these cows? How long would she have to hold out?

13 GEORGE'S ENTERTAINMENT

As night approached, the blizzard grew more powerful. Snow sifted up through the cracks in the schoolhouse floor. Wind pounded the building mercilessly. A thick layer of frost formed along the inside wall farthest from the stove, which was being stoked with fuel every hour. The damper was opened as far as Miss Brophy dared, and yet there was barely enough heat to warm the room.

At six o'clock, Miss Brophy spread a blanket in front of the stove. "Now, everyone, have a seat. Be sure to keep on your coats and caps. We don't want anyone to catch cold on our picnic," she said brightly.

"A picnic?" Donald Feeney asked incredulously.

"We're having a picnic dinner. Let's check our lunch pails to see what might be left."

All that could be found was one butter sandwich. Miss

Brophy used oysters, canned corn, milk, and rice to make a kind of stew. While the helpings were small, no one complained. For dessert, Miss Brophy gave the children a surprise — half a sugar cookie each. She had made the cookies for the Christmas program.

"What time is it?" Lucia Hebbert asked when they had eaten.

"Nearly bedtime," Miss Brophy replied. She shot a worried glance at the red-hot stove and the stovepipe, which had not been cleaned since the week before. A smokestack filled with too much soot might easily catch fire. "Girls, you will sleep on the benches. George, help me push them together. The gentlemen will have to sleep on the floor. Keep your hats, coats, scarves, and mittens on. We only have two blankets — just enough for the youngest children to share."

Since it was too dangerous to go to the outhouse, everyone used an old bucket Miss Brophy put in a corner screened off with a blanket hung over a rope. When all the children were ready for bed, Miss Brophy blew out the lamp. She did not want to use up any more kerosene. The only light was from the flickering fire in the stove. The Christmas decorations on the tree danced and shimmered as the schoolhouse swayed. The creaking noises kept the children fearful and awake.

"What time is it?" Lucia whined again.

"I want to go home," Lucy Hoopes sobbed.

"I want my mama," Maude Hoopes said tearfully.

"Does anyone see the elephant on the ceiling?" George interrupted. He was lying on his back with his fingers laced behind his head, staring up at the shadows dancing on the ceiling. "See how he wiggles his ears?"

The children laughed and began talking all at once.

"There goes a big wagon," Donald Feeney said.

"What about that one? It's a skunk, I bet," Fred Falkenberg shouted.

"Hold your nose!" George said, and all the children held their noses.

"I see dancing ladies," Lucy Hoopes said shyly.

"I see summertime," Lorenzo Hebbert blurted. "That's the big grass moving, and it's hot. It's July."

"I wish it were summer again," Myra Renshaw said longingly.

"Me, too."

"Well, I'm thinking of summer. Can you guess what I'm thinking?" George said. The other children were listening so attentively that only George noticed Miss Brophy nervously checking the stovepipe. "You do this only in summertime and you have to be quick. What is it, Fred?"

"Jumping over railroad tracks?"

"No."

"Throwing lit matches?" Donald Feeney suggested.

137

"No."

"Frog catching?"

"Right!" George said, and laughed. "Who wants to be next? Lucia, what do you like to do when it's a hot summer day?"

"Well, I like to go down into the root cellar under the soddy 'cause it's cool and dark. I play with my corn dolls, and they have fancy parties."

"Fancy parties! That's not what *I* like," Lorenzo Hebbert said. "I like Fourth of July and going into Scotland and drinking lemonade and watching the old blue Union soldier boys shoot their guns. And I like to buy that sticky string candy, if I got a penny. I balance on the rail and watch the horse races and I eats and eats till I puke."

Everyone laughed again. It wasn't so bad lying on the cold, drafty schoolhouse floor when they could pretend it was really July and blazing hot. Miss Brophy smiled at George. He smiled himself. He had never realized how clever he could be at entertaining people.

"George," Myra said eagerly, "tell us a story. Tell us a real exciting adventure story."

"All right," George said, and he told Addie's story about the runaway elephant. He added his own details, telling how the elephant came to town and frightened everyone but the children, of course, who jumped on his back and went for a ride up and down Main Street. By the time George had finished, Lena and Lucia were asleep, curled up together. Arnold and his brother Simon were snoring away peacefully. Even Maude and Lucy Hoopes were nodding their heads. They were too tired to be frightened any longer.

George was fearful and homesick, but he didn't say it. He was worried about his sister. Even though Miss Brophy reassured him that Addie was safe, somehow he knew deep down that she had not made it home. What could he do? He couldn't go out on his own and tell Pa.

George lay awake most of the night, anxiously watching the shadows. He wondered what Mother must be thinking. Were his brothers worried about him? Maybe nobody at home was asleep, either. Maybe they were just sitting in the dark, too, waiting for the blizzard to stop howling.

At last he dozed. Suddenly, he woke up with a start, his arm cramped and tingling from the weight of his head. There was Miss Brophy, checking the stovepipe again. She was worried, he could tell. If the schoolhouse caught on fire, where would they go? They'd all be swallowed up in snow and wind. George was so tired he couldn't think clearly. Yet he tried his best to keep his eyes open. Shouldn't he stay awake and help Miss Brophy watch that stovepipe? Shouldn't he make sure she did not fall asleep, too? His eyes shut just for a moment. He drifted off.

The next morning, the blizzard continued to rage. Miss

Brophy forced the door open and scooped up several buckets of snow to melt for cooking and washing. She used the snow water with the last of the condensed milk to make hot cocoa for breakfast. Each child also had a piece of bread and two slices of canned peach.

While Fred Falkenberg and Emma Schuler washed the cocoa pan and spoons, Miss Brophy put on the snowshoes and went outside with a rope around her waist to bring in four more buckets of coal. "I gave Nell some more hay," she told George breathlessly when she returned, covered with snow.

The storm boomed all day long. The children kept busy cleaning the classroom and doing their lessons. When they had recess, George pushed all the benches and tables to one side and led everyone in a strange prairie-chicken dance he invented. It felt good to get up and move around and jump and holler.

In the afternoon, the children sang Christmas carols. Miss Brophy showed how to weave mats with strips of paper. To make the mats more decorative, she suggested drawing pictures on the paper strips before they started weaving. George covered his paper strips with leaping antelopes. When everyone was finished, they played hide-the-button.

It was early evening, and no parents had come. The wind bellowed just as loudly as ever. George wondered what Miss Brophy would think of to do next.

"What time is it?" Lucia demanded for the hundredth time.

"Five-thirty," Miss Brophy said. "Time for dinner."

Nobody seemed happy about another meal of oysters. Since the milk was gone, there could be no stew. Instead, Miss Brophy gave each child oysters, two crackers, and a spoonful of apple cobbler. Some held their noses as they swallowed the slippery grey oysters. They were all hungry when dinner was finished, but nobody complained because nobody wanted more oysters.

The children were tired from having had so little rest the night before. All fell asleep quickly, except for George. "Should I go out to the shed and get more coal?" he asked sleepily.

"It's not safe outdoors now, George," Miss Brophy replied quietly. "Drifts may have covered the shed door."

"We could dig a passage," George suggested.

"That might take hours. Why don't you try and get some rest? We have enough coal for tonight."

George curled up on the hard, cold floor, stuffing his cap beneath his head for a scratchy pillow. Would the morning ever come? Would he ever feel warm and comfortable again? He shivered and shut his eyes.

George woke up, then squinted. For the second morning in a row, he didn't know where he was. Why was it so quiet? Had Pa let him sleep late? And why did Mother have the kerosene lamp burning so brightly?

He rubbed his eyes. He wasn't home. He was on the schoolroom floor. There was no kerosene lamp. The light he saw was from the sun shining through the classroom's ice-glazed windows.

The sun!

George scrambled to his feet. The roaring storm had finally ended. He couldn't help himself — he let out a yelp and woke everyone. Laughing giddily, Fred Falkenberg and George did the prairie-chicken dance again. Soon they would all be rescued! Everyone, even Miss Brophy, cheered.

While the children ate a breakfast of the last sugar cookies, crackers, and melted snow water, they heard a loud thumping against the wall. Miss Brophy hurried to try the door, but the drift outside blocked the way. She tugged at the window. It was frozen shut. Finally, with George's help, she managed to pry it open. A man covered with snow and ice slid inside. Miss Brophy quickly shut the window as a frigid blast whipped through the room.

At first no one recognized him. His forehead and eyes were caked with ice, his beard was frozen, and his face was nearly purple from walking in the intense cold. He was wearing snowshoes and carrying a bundle under his arm. "Is everyone safe?" the man said. "I've brought some food and a blanket or two."

"Pa!" George shouted, and ran to his father's arms.

"Are you all right? We were so worried," Pa said, giving him a huge hug. "Where's your sister? Where's Addie?"

The room was suddenly silent. Miss Brophy's face went pale. "She...she didn't make it home?"

"No," Pa replied, his voice tight. "We haven't seen her since she and George left for school, two days ago."

Miss Brophy lowered herself slowly onto a bench. "She went to Ree Heights. She went to deliver a message to Tilla Bergstrom's family the morning before the storm. She should have made it there before it broke. She may be there still..."

"God willing," Pa said under his breath. He pulled a dry muffler from inside the bundle and wrapped it around his face. "I'll try and bring in some more coal for you from the shed. Then I'm going out to find Addie. The wind's bitter. Don't let anyone go outside."

"Pa, let me go with you to find Addie," George begged as his father prepared to leave through the window.

Pa paused.

"He can borrow my snowshoes," Miss Brophy said. "And there are certainly enough mittens, caps, and scarves here to keep George warm."

"All right, George. If you can get ready quickly enough," Pa said. "I'm sure I can use your help."

14 OLD NO HORN

By the second night of the storm, Addie had done everything possible to keep from falling asleep. She had fed and milked the cows and had given each one handfuls of snow that had drifted into the barn. Since she couldn't find a pail, most of the milk went to waste. Addie pretended to be one of Grandpa's cats back in Sabula. Whenever Grandpa had milked, he shot a stream into the air. The clever barn cats never missed a drop. Addie leaned over, opened her mouth, and pulled "Old No Horn's" teat. A small, warm stream of milk squirted her face. After several more tries, she aimed correctly.

When she wasn't taking care of the cows, she marched and sang "My Country 'Tis Of Thee." She shouted at the top of her lungs, although she knew the wind was roaring so loudly no one outside could hear her. She tried spelling all the states she could remember. She chanted the first, middle, and last names of all her cousins back in Iowa.

For what she thought was only a few moments, she dozed off. Fortunately, a lowing, hungry cow woke her. "Breakfast time! Let's go, Ruby Lillian," Addie said, and climbed up into the loft to pitch more hay down.

Addie sang Christmas carols to the cows while they ate. When she ran out of songs, she told stories. She recited her poem, "The Wild Prairie Rose," a dozen times. She even tried to place a sleeping duck on each of her feet for warmth, but the ducks did not like this idea and waddled away.

Addie felt as if she and Ruby Lillian had been in this barn forever, and still there was no sign of a rescue. She peered out a crack in the door but could see only thick, whirling snow. Maybe the barn was too far to be reached from the farmer's house. What if the farmer had tried with a long rope, but the rope broke? What if...

To keep from thinking about the poor, frozen, lost farmer, she stamped her feet two hundred times and beat her hands together. Night and a whole day had come and gone. It was night again, and the storm still screamed. How long could it last?

Addie thought of Tilla and Tilla's mother and felt miserable and sick at heart. She thought of Miss Brophy and hoped no one else from the class had been caught in the blizzard going home. She tried to picture Mother's face. She thought about George. She pictured Pa. He looked troubled.

"What if Pa's lost, Ruby Lillian? What if he tries to come looking for us and loses his way?"

A thousand anxious thoughts raced through her mind. Back and forth she paced, flapping her numb arms against her body. The barn seemed to be growing colder and colder. Her stockings were wet, and her feet chafed and itched from chilblains. Her legs were stiff. Her bruised knees ached from her earlier fall on the ice. She had nibbled the last small bit of bread long ago. Although there was plenty of milk, she longed for a real meal. She put her ear to the door crack and heard no sleigh bells, no voices, nothing except screaming wind.

"Of course the storm will end," she said, holding her doll tight. "No blizzard lasts forever. As long as the cows are fed and don't freeze to death, I'll have a small bit of milk. I won't starve. All I have to do is stay awake and keep moving...keep moving and stay awake...stay awake and keep moving."

Addie climbed up and down the ladder a dozen times, for something new to do. More than anything else, she wanted to drift into sleep in the soft hay.

Finally, discouraged and exhausted, she crawled into the stall beside Old No Horn. After two days without being mucked out, the stall was filthy. Addie laid armfuls of clean hay on the floor. Immediately, the lumbering cow folded up its legs and lay down. It lowed mournfully, sounding as hopeless as Addie felt.

"Don't give up, Old No Horn," she mumbled, leaning against the cow's broad, warm side. She held Ruby Lillian snug inside her pocket. Old No Horn's tail flapped back and forth, back and forth. "Think of lovely summer pastures. Green, green grass everywhere. Not just old dry hay. And it's warm. The flies are buzzing. Remember flies? And you flap your tail. Flap. Flap. Flap."

Her head nodded. She felt almost warm now. Maybe it was easier to sleep. Wasn't death just like taking a nap? That's how Tilla's mother and baby looked. Sleeping. So peacefully.

Addie did not know how long she drowsed. Suddenly, her eyes shot open. She mustn't sleep. She *mustn't*. Desperately, she rolled to her knees and staggered to her feet. She could hear a flapping noise. Was it Old No Horn's tail flapping as she dreamt? "Wake up, Old No Horn! Do you hear me, WAKE UP! You'll die if you fall asleep!" she shouted.

The noise became louder. But it wasn't Old No Horn's tail — it was the door. *There was someone at the door.*

With a terrific crash, the barn door swung wide open. Light flooded inside. "Who's there?" a man's voice called.

"Anybody in here? I heard a voice, Mother. I think there's somebody in here!"

A bundled, dark shape stood in the doorway. It came closer. Addie squinted. She held her hands over her face.

"You're scaring her, Hiram. Stop shouting and see to the cows. Here, sweet child," a woman's kind voice said. "Put this around your shoulders. Don't be afraid. You're safe now. Can you imagine, Hiram? The poor thing's been out here in our barn for Heaven knows how long."

Someone was wrapping something around her. Someone was picking her up. Addie gripped Ruby Lillian as she was carried outside. The light was very bright and blinding; it must be morning, she thought. Where are we going?

Bitter-cold wind whipped around her as she was carried through huge drifts to a soddy nearly covered by a mountain of snow. Inside, three boys stared and stared at her. Their hair was so red it nearly hurt her eyes.

"Now come in, poor dearie. Set her here, Hiram, on this chair — not too close to the stove," the woman said, pulling another blanket around Addie.

The woman poured warm water from a tea kettle into two snow-filled basins, then mixed the water and lowered her own arm in to make sure the temperature was right.

Gently, she pulled off Addie's boots and socks and submerged her feet in the basin on the floor. "Put your hands in the other basin, child," she instructed. Addie winced. Her skin felt as if it was on fire.

"That's a brave girl. Now let's see how we're doing. Very nicely. Very nicely. Your skin is pink. That's good."

The woman carefully lifted Addie's feet from the basin and wrapped them in a towel and a blanket. She pulled another chair nearby so that Addie could rest her feet in an elevated position. Then she carefully dried and wrapped Addie's hands. Even though the woman was gentle, blisters immediately formed all over Addie's hands and legs and feet. The skin on her nose and ears and neck burned painfully.

"How is she?" the man asked.

"The frostbite's not so bad," the woman replied. She carefully dabbed Addie's face and neck with something thick and white and soothing. "I'll put some of this salve on her blisters. She's going to hurt for a while. But she won't lose any fingers or toes. How are the cows? Will they live?"

"They appear to be in good condition, thanks to this little lady. She must know a thing or two about taking care of cows," the man said, and smiled at Addie. "I'm Hiram McMasters, and this is my wife, Julia. And what might your name be?" He offered Addie a spoonful of hot tea. She could not hold the spoon herself because her hands were wrapped in blankets.

"Addie Mills," she said, and took an eager sip. The three

boys, who were introduced as Magnus, Robert, and Hiram, Jr., still stared. Each was slightly taller than the next. Their mouths were half-opened in the same sagging *O*-shapes.

"Leave the child be, boys. Look at her, she's fairly ready to collapse," their mother said. "She needs to eat and rest. Maybe you boys can help your father connect a good stout rope between the house and the barn. Then maybe next time there's a bad blizzard, we'll be able to do the milking and feeding."

"That wind was too strong to let anyone go wandering alone — even across the barnyard," her husband replied. "It's a miracle this poor, wee mite was there to save our cows. A real miracle."

Mrs. McMasters stood up and bustled about in a take-charge way, preparing a heaping plate of hot food.

"You look awful," Magnus McMasters whispered to Addie.

Even though every part of her throbbed with pain, Addie made a grin she hoped looked frightening. His rude comment was reassuring and familiar, like something one of her own pesky brothers would say.

"How did you stay all that time in our cold barn while the storm was blowing?" demanded Robert, the second biggest boy.

"*Nisser.* It was the *nisser* who saved me," Addie whispered mysteriously. She leaned closer, aware that her salve-smeared

150

face must appear eerie and otherworldly. "Haven't you ever heard of the *nisser* who live in your barn? They're little people with pointed red hats and wooden shoes. Everyone knows about them. They saved my life."

The boys looked at each other, wide-eyed. Their little O-shaped lips collapsed. Addie chuckled. She unwrapped one hand slightly, grasped a fork, and shoveled fried salt pork and potatoes into her mouth.

15   CALICO
IN THE COTTONWOOD

The blizzard cleared, but the drifts around Oak Hollow were still so high that only the very tips of the cottonwood trees could be seen. A week after the storm, George insisted on climbing up the deepest pile in the new snowshoes Pa had made. He wanted to tie a long fluttering piece of turkey-red calico on a limb.

"Why are you doing that?" Addie called, all bundled in her coat and her best apron. "George, come down! We're going to be late for the school program."

"Just a minute," George replied, fastening the cloth exactly at the drift's crest. He leapt down in giant, awkward steps. "Now when summer comes, we'll remember exactly how high the snow was. All we'll have to do is look up at that turkey red and we'll know."

"When summer comes! Only you would think of such

a thing, George," Addie said, and smiled. She gave his mule-ear cap an affectionate tug, remembering how happy she had been to see George and Pa when they arrived in the sleigh at the McMasters' house. They had searched for ten long hours. She would never forget the look of joy on Pa's face or the way George whooped and hollered, "O Come All Ye Faithful" all three miles to Oak Hollow. George said he sang just to let Mother, Burt, Lew, Nellie May, and the rest of the world know that Addie was coming home, safe and sound — just in time for Christmas dinner.

Addie put up her hands to shield her eyes and squinted at the red material dancing in the breeze. The blizzard seemed like a bad dream — a scary story someone had once told her that she'd now half-forgotten. Summer would come again, and life would be even finer than it was at this very fine moment.

"Come on, you two!" Pa called from the sleigh. Mother, Lew, Burt, and Nellie May were already snug in blankets and coats and a big buffalo robe. The sun shone brightly this afternoon, and the air was clear and cold.

"Wheeee!" Lew shouted as the sleigh glided over the snow. "I can taste the wind! It makes my teeth feel fuzzy!"

"Sit down, Lew, before you fall out!" Pa said.

Everything looked different. Addie wasn't sure if it were the snow that had changed the landscape or if she were just seeing things in a new way. The route to the schoolhouse had never seemed so fascinating before. Even George kept looking all around, expectant and excited.

At the schoolyard there were wagons and cutters of all kinds. Smoke was pouring from the chimney, and Addie could smell something delicious cooking. She helped her youngest brothers to the ground while Pa tied the horses. She held Burt's and Lew's hands tightly, not so much to keep them from running away as to steady herself. She was so nervous that she felt as if she might float away. It was reassuring to know Ruby Lillian was in her pocket.

The schoolhouse was crowded with people, all smiling and shaking hands, glad to see each other. Anna and Mr. Fency gave each of the Mills children an affectionate hug. Even Mr. and Mrs. McMasters were there with their red-haired sons. The boys waved shyly.

The classroom had been transformed. Candles glowed on the Christmas tree, making the other decorations flicker magically. Lew and Burt ran to the tree and stared as if they had never seen anything so marvelous in their lives.

"Come meet my teacher," Addie begged. But the little boys refused to budge. They stood completely still, admiring the candy in little bags, the dancing ships, and the beautiful glittering stars.

"Where did the tree come from?" Burt whispered. "How'd you get it to stay like that?"

Miss Brophy laughed. "Hello, Addie. Are these your little brothers?" Her teacher looked even lovelier than usual. She was wearing a soft green dress with a small sprig of holly on her collar.

Lew and Burt immediately hid behind their sister's skirt.

"I know you'll do a wonderful job reciting your poem. Good luck," Miss Brophy said. She hurriedly kissed the top of Addie's head and went to the front of the room to announce that the program would soon begin.

"Oh, ugh!" Lew hissed. "If that lady's ever my teacher, she better not try to kiss me."

Addie laughed and gave her brother a hug. He yelped defiantly and wriggled free.

"Would all the parents please take their seats now?" Miss Brophy said in a loud voice. "All the children can come to the front and sit on the floor.

"We have many reasons to come together today. Not only are we gathered to celebrate the holiday season, we are here to show our thanks for surviving the terrible blizzard without tragedy."

"Amen," said someone in the crowd. "Thank the Lord."

The schoolhouse door swung open. Addie could not see the latecomers until they moved shyly forward along the wall. It was Tilla and her brother, Ole. Excitedly, Addie waved, but she did not catch Tilla's attention.

"One of our students, Addie Mills," Miss Brophy continued, "courageously survived two nights and nearly two days of the blizzard in a barn all by herself."

The audience craned their necks to see where Addie stood. She blushed.

"We were fortunate not to lose any students to the cold and the snow. Your children spent the time in the schoolhouse with few complaints — though I can tell you that they were tired of oysters and crackers!"

Everyone laughed.

"Our thanks and a special award for bravery goes to one person whose help was invaluable to me throughout the storm. He kept up the children's spirits as well as mine. Will George Mills please step forward?"

The children clapped and cheered while George, red-faced and surprised, walked to the front of the room. Miss Brophy pinned a blue ribbon trimmed with shimmering gold to his shirt.

Everyone applauded. Now George smiled, his back straight and tall. Addie thought her brother looked every bit a hero. She clapped proudly. George was so delighted by the audience's reaction that he quickly repinned his splendid ribbon upside down and, to everyone's shock and amazement, walked across the front of the room on his hands! The crowd cheered wildly.

George dusted himself off and took a seat on the side of the room, glowing with triumph.

The presentation of verse and Christmas carols was performed without any major mishap. Addie recited her poem and did not forget any of the words. Emma and Gunther Schuler performed "O Tannenbaum" in German followed by "Oh Christmas Tree" in English. Fred Falkenberg demonstrated how to spell *perambulator* and *chemistry* without faltering. And just as it said on the program, Tilla Bergstrom sang, "I Am So Glad Each Christmas Eve" in Norwegian. Addie noticed Miss Brophy dabbing her eyes with her handkerchief when Tilla finished.

When the program ended, the students and Miss Brophy bowed together. The children did not waste any time getting in line to receive Christmas cookies decorated with pink icing.

"I'm very happy you came, Tilla," Addie said, nervously breaking her cookie into small pieces. "I'm sorry I left your house so quickly without telling you the real reason I came."

"Da real reason?" Tilla asked.

"I wanted to apologize for what happened with those horrible Connolly boys. I wanted to tell you I was sorry for the lie I told, the way I got you in trouble with them. And I —"

"I *vas* mad," Tilla interrupted softly, "but I already forgives you."

"You do?"

Tilla nodded.

Addie smiled, filled with relief. She was glad she did not have to explain any further. Tilla had understood exactly what she had meant. And for the first time, Addie appreciated the strength and wisdom of her friend — the only one brave and bold enough to ride on deck from Norway with sea wind blowing in her face. So many people depended on Tilla. Her family. Miss Brophy. And me, Addie thought. I need Tilla, too.

"I've been thinking," Addie continued, "Tilla, you don't have to stop learning just because you can't come back to school."

Tilla looked confused.

"Don't you see? I can teach you. Every week, you can come to my house. I know Miss Brophy would let me borrow a reader. Or maybe Anna Fency will lend me one of her books. And that way we can still see each other, if your Pa can spare you. What do you say, Tilla?"

There was something familiar about the way Tilla held her chin, the way her eyes flashed with defiance. "But vill I haff to call you Miss Mills?"

"No," Addie said, and laughed. "You can call me whatever you want as long as you don't say *'pokkers ta deg!'*"

Now it was Tilla's turn to laugh. It was the old Tilla roar, rude and loud and imperfect. And wonderful. At last, the moment Addie had been waiting for had arrived. "I want you to meet someone, Tilla. Someone very fine. I hope you will like her. I've already told her all about you." Addie carefully pulled out Ruby Lillian. "You can hold her. Go ahead."

Tilla didn't say anything. She took the doll gingerly, examining two dainty hands and an impossibly small, curved smile. With her finger, Tilla outlined her beautiful ringlets, one at a time, murmuring, "She is so *livaktig*. How do you say? She is so alife!"

"She has another dress I made for everyday and a matching bonnet. I'll show it to you sometime. This is her good dress — the one she wears for parties and special occasions," Addie said proudly.

Tilla was so absorbed in admiring the doll that she did not seem to be listening. She handed Ruby Lillian back tenderly, as if she were a real, breathing person.

Addie shook her head. Ruby Lillian had helped Addie through hard times. Now she could help Tilla, too. "No. You can take Ruby Lillian home and play with her for as many days as you like."

"I can?" Tilla whispered in disbelief. "You vill let me?"

"Of course. After all, aren't we best friends?" Addie said, and watched joy dance and gleam in Tilla's eyes like the silver foil stars on Miss Brophy's Christmas tree.